FORGED

EDGE: Book Three of The Golden Trilogy
Copyright © 2018 by K.M. Robinson.

Published by Crescent Sea Publishing.
www.crescentseapublishing.com

Cover designed by Reading Transforms.
Image copyright © K.M. Robinson Photography.
Interior graphics by Millennium Genesis.

This is a work of fiction. Names, characters, brands, trademarks, places, and incidents either are the product of the author's imagination or are used fictitiously. Any resemblance to actual events, locales, organizations, or persons, living or dead, is entirely coincidental and beyond the intent of either the author or the publisher.

FORGED

K.M. ROBINSON

Crescent Sea
PUBLISHING

To those who have found themselves in situations that were less than ideal, and handled them with grace and courage anyway.

The story of Goldilocks hits a few of the main parts of my tale, but my story started long before I met the Baers.

When people neglect to tell the part about me being sent on a mission to destroy the Baer family, they also forget to mention my training, my manipulative cousin, my overbearing mentor, and that I was a vicious fighter.

My name is Auluria, but once upon a time, I was a young girl known as Lur. This is the story of how that deceptive girl known as Goldilocks came to be.

Chapter 1

W *hap!*

I fell hard on my backside.

"Get up," his voice commanded.

I tried to sit up, but pain shot through my back.

"Get up, we have work to do," he demanded again.

"I'm trying," I said through gritted teeth.

Shadoe was quite possibly my least favorite person. It had only been a week since my aunt had died and my cousin, Lowell, had brought me into his group of fighters where he was working to end the corrupt Society we lived in. I was lucky I had a cousin to care for me at all. I had lost my parents and my aunt; Lowell was the only family I had left.

Shadoe reached down to me and pulled me to my feet. Stepping back, he paused as I took a breath of air. Before I could even gasp, he launched himself at me yet again, pummeling me to the ground.

I shrieked as I hit the dirt, brown dusty particles covering my forearms and hands. Lowell stood several yards away raising his eyebrow at me. *I was weak* and he didn't like it.

"*Lur*," Shadoe said, using the name I so despised.

"That is *not* my name," I growled.

"Get it right." He scowled.

I hated him.

But Lowell would not save me.

He paired me with Shadoe; a man who had been born to work with Lowell. His father before him worked with my cousin, until his death a few years before, and now Shadoe was his right-hand man.

I rose to my feet, determined not to fall again. Raising a hand in front of me, I protected my face like Shadoe had shown me. He threw a punch and I blocked it with one hand, then swept my foot around the back of his leg and pulled his knee out.

He faltered and I slammed the heel of my hand into his jaw, forcing him back.

I knew Lowell was watching, so I continued my attack. Punching him in the stomach, Shadoe fell to his knees. I took the opportunity to bring my knee up, connecting it with his face. As I did, he gripped my leg; I once again landed on the ground. I struggled for air as he wrapped his hands around my throat. It hurt, but he didn't cut off my air supply.

"Better," he said, releasing me.

"You're improving, Auluria," Lowell commented as he walked over to us. He motioned for me to follow him. I was grateful for the reprieve.

"I know this has not been an easy transition for you, Auluria, but I appreciate that you are making the effort. I know Shadoe is training you hard, but it's only because I want you to survive. This fight that we are in is not easy. I won't send you out there unprepared."

"I'm trying," I said weakly.

"I know you are." He nodded. "You just have to *keep* trying. You did better today. But now that you are doing better, he's going to push you harder. It won't seem like it's getting any easier, even though you are improving each day. Don't get discouraged."

We walked along through the field toward the trees.

I wished Lowell would spend more time with me. We were never close, but at least when I was a child, he'd spend time playing with me. Now he only spoke to me when necessary. He let Shadoe oversee everything I did.

"Auluria, you know what we're doing is the right thing, don't you?" Lowell asked, his words drawn out.

"I do," I said with measured breath.

We continued forward to his temporary shelter. Lowell's group had a transient nature to it. They were always moving from place to place. They never stayed still for long. All of the housing was short term. We lived in the woods, in fields, and, on occasion, we spent a few nights in an actual home.

I never did understand why Lowell chose this over his parents' home. It sat abandoned in town since Lowell had taken me in. I missed the walls and the protection the small house offered. I missed the privacy.

"The government needs to be destroyed and reestablished," Lowell continued, sitting down in front of a fire. "You are smart, Auluria; once you finish your training, I know you will be a great asset to our campaign. I can see you rising in the ranks quickly. Even as a child, you were very good at problem-solving."

His lips tugged up just a touch as he remembered our childhood games. My own followed suit as I stretched a hand out toward the fire. The evenings were cool, and as we sat in the twilight I could feel the sweat on my skin take a frosty turn. I shifted closer to the fire.

"I'll do my best, Lowell," I assured him.

I hated the idea of fighting. I didn't like that I needed to be trained. But I also wanted to be prepared. I knew what happened to girls like me if the Society caught us alone.

We lived in a place that was haunted by threats from

foreign nations. Our government gave them our food and resources to secure safety and protection, but it wasn't enough. They demanded more, and the more they demanded, the more the Society took from its people. A wall was constructed around the nation to protect it, keeping invaders at bay. The people were left with barely enough to survive. Like the fire in front of me, the nations only grew, demanding everything in their paths. The government wanted an army to defeat our enemies. The boys were sent to training camps to learn to fight while the girls that were captured were sent to breeding camps to further populate the country. Orphans were taken first, then young people, then anyone the soldiers found alone that could be easily overtaken.

I knew learning to fight would give me the power to protect myself, so I tolerated my lessons with Shadoe. I also knew Lowell was protecting me and I needed to help him. I wanted to stop the government too; the government that had destroyed us all.

"Auluria, Shadoe is doing a good job training you. I know it isn't easy right now, but trust me, it's for the best."

"I know Lowell, I trust you."

I saw his eyes brighten, the skin on his face tightening as he suppressed a grin. "Good."

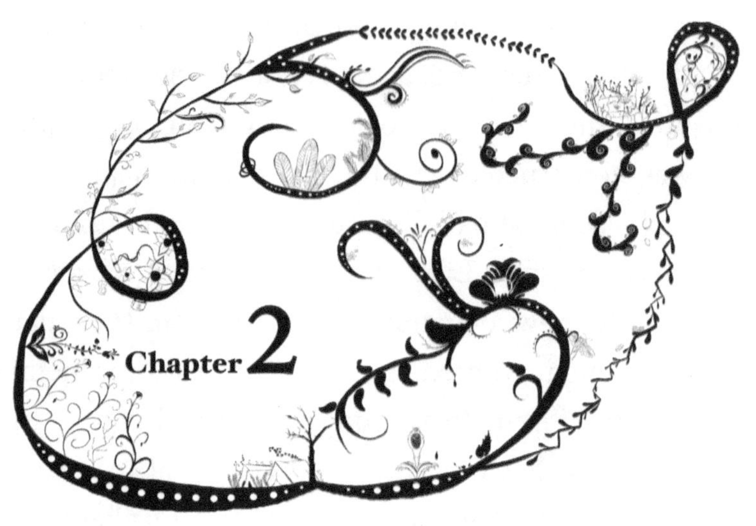

Chapter 2

"You have to be faster than that," Shadoe shouted as I dangled from a tree. "You can't take your time climbing. You have to be sure of yourself. If you need to evade your enemy, you must be quick."

"And silent, and cunning. I know," I said sarcastically. "I have the words down, Shadoe; it's the putting into practice part that's the problem."

"Get down," he demanded.

The last thing I wanted was to be too slow again, so I released my hands and dropped. I shouldn't have from the height I was at, but the shooting pain in my ankle subsided quickly enough.

"I've had enough of tree climbing for today, follow

me," Shadoe said gruffly after demonstrating a flawless climb once again.

We walked through the forest and into a marshy area. The grass was tall, wild and unruly. Frogs jumped away as we approached.

"Take your clothes off and get in," he said.

I looked at him, horrified.

"Well, go on, we don't have all day."

"But—" I started.

"Move it!" he insisted.

I pulled my dress over my head once he turned his back to me, leaving my under clothes in place. The nights had been cool and the water felt too cold against my skin. I held my gasp in so Shadoe couldn't criticize me.

"Swim," he ordered once he heard me enter the water.

He watched as I swam laps back and forth from one end of the pond to the other. After what seemed an eternity I saw him slip into the water behind me. I swam away as he stepped in.

When I turned back around, he was watching me. I swam in his direction, waiting for instructions. Instead of him speaking to me, the water told me what to do next: fight for my life.

Shadoe held me under the water. He stood over me and forced me into a shallow, watery grave. I planted my feet against the bottom and pushed upward as hard as I could. My skull slammed into his jaw, but he propelled me back down. I sputtered in my seconds above the water, trying to inhale as much air as possible.

His strong arms held me down, burying my feet in the mud below. I reached up and scratched at his hands, but it didn't seem to faze him. Turning my head to the side, I bit down hard on his knuckles. I could hear his angry words under the water.

When even that didn't work, I held still. I let my body go limp and forced the panic from my thoughts. Waiting, I let the air bubble from my lips, only retaining a bit in my lungs. They burned as I forced myself not to move. I thought I would die.

I held still long enough to scare Shadoe. He pulled me from the water, but I remained motionless. I resisted the urge to gasp for air, though I desperately needed it. Shadoe shook me, still holding my shoulders. I could feel the terrified look creep over his face, even though I couldn't see with my eyes closed. The muscles tensed in his hands around me.

When he threw me over his shoulder, I gasped for air, taking a deep gulp. The crashing water prevented him from hearing my breath. Holding still again I let him rush me toward the shore.

"Shadoe!" I heard Lowell shout in the distance. His rapidly approaching footsteps told me he was running toward us and he was nervous I was hurt.

My instructor set me down on the ground far too

hard. He leaned down to me and felt for breath. I stilled my lungs, satisfied that I would worry him.

"Auluria?" He sounded scared. He tapped my face as Lowell drew closer.

"*Auluria?*" Shadoe repeated. Panic set in.

As he leaned back down to check for a pulse, I kicked my leg up over him, knocking him off balance. My hand caught his face, sending his head backward. As he recoiled, I pulled my knee toward my body and forced it out, kicking him as hard as I could in the face. The noise that came from him was terrifying and I suddenly felt terrible for tricking him like that.

He fell back into the pond, unconscious. I left him there for Lowell to fish out of the water. I knew I should stay and apologize, but in that moment, he was the man who tried to drown me, and I hated him.

I stomped back to the camp.

"That was cruel," Lowell said later that night.

"He tried to drown me," I objected.

"He was training you."

"By killing me?" My rage had only grown since I left the marsh.

"Yes," Lowell's answer surprised me. "If you knew

everything he was going to do before he did it, you'd always be prepared. The enemy isn't going to warn you before they strike. You need to be prepared to handle those situations."

It made sense, in a twisted kind of way.

"But, *Missy*," now he was angry, "No more knocking him out. Teach him a lesson, *show off* if you want; take him down a peg or two for all I care, but I need him *conscious* and functioning. Do you understand?"

"I understand."

"Shadoe is a good teacher," he softened "And a good man. You'll learn to trust him in time."

"I should apologize," I relented.

"Yes, you should," Lowell said, a little too quickly. I didn't like that he sided with Shadoe over his own cousin.

I wandered through the field we were camping in. We were far out in the wastelands by the edge of the woods where the Society wouldn't bother us. I wove my way around the rest of Lowell's flock until I found Shadoe sitting by a fire, a mug in his hand.

Sitting down beside him, I decided not speak. Shadoe made no effort to talk either. The silence surrounded us and I listened to the fire snap.

"Water?" he asked after fifteen minutes had passed. He held his mug out to me.

I shook my head.

"I'm sorry I knocked you out today," I said unhappily.

He didn't respond.

"I know you're trying to help," I added.

"You need to be able to protect yourself. I'm only trying to help you do that," he said.

"I know," I patronized.

"You're a good fighter," Shadoe added as the fire sparked and hissed at us. "Just… inexperienced. Once you've done this for a bit, you could be as good as any of the men here. You're a fighter, Lur."

"Why do you keep calling me that?"

"Because I know you hate it," he shrugged. "It motivates you to prove me wrong. And Auluria is so *feminine* sounding—*Lur* is stronger. Not to mention it's shorter." He actually grinned at the last comment. It was the first time I'd ever seen him do anything but scowl.

I smiled. "I still hate it."

"And you still hate *me*. I get it," he concluded. "But at least you're getting better."

He held his mug out to me again, insisting I drink. I started to reach for it, but stopped.

"You're not going to attack me again, are you?" I asked, pulling back my hand.

"No." He half grinned. "We're taking the night off, Lur. Take it," he nodded to the mug.

True to his word, I was not attacked.

The water felt good on my throat. The fire cast an

orange glow on us as its flames danced. We sat in silence for a while longer before I finally rose.

"I should get back," I said, handing him the mug.

He nodded, turning back to the fire as I left. He never watched me walk away. A gentleman would have made sure I arrived at home—or *temporary home*—safely. Shadoe didn't care.

Chapter 3

"What am I supposed to do with this?" I asked, a tremble in my voice.

I held a cold, metal knife in my hands. I prayed I wouldn't have to use it on some poor, unassuming animal.

"Throw it," Shadoe said. "Like this."

He raised his hands in the air, one for balance and one for aim. The knife sailed through the air and buried itself deep into a tree trunk.

"Now you." He motioned to the knife I held.

I mimicked his pose, spacing myself out just as he had. I balanced myself with my left hand, holding the knife tightly in my right. I watched my stationary target; a nearby tree. Stepping forward, I raised the knife and propelled it toward the trunk. It landed in the bark with a satisfying thud. I turned to look at Shadoe triumphantly.

"And you even breathed correctly when you released it." He almost sounded impressed.

"I watched you," I said, indicating I noted his exact movements as he demonstrated.

"Well, Lur, it looks like you are finally learning," he nodded appreciatively. I was finally starting to make some headway with the stoic man.

"Do it again. This time, hit *here*."

He made a mark on the tree, a target for me to focus on.

I raised my arms and released my weapon. It found its mark several inches below Shadoe's indentation.

"At least it hit the tree," he said. The anger of the first few weeks of training could no longer be found in his voice.

Over the last few weeks since the incident in the water, we found our stride. He no longer yelled at me and I no longer despised him as much. He talked to me and I talked back. Shadoe explained calmly and rationally; I understood and put it into practice. We were cool to each other, but no longer harsh.

Raising my hands, I threw the knife again. This time it landed closer to my target. My fourth try hit with the wrong side and bounced off, sending me skittering backward to avoid being hit. Shadoe made me practice for two hours. My arms were sore, but I pushed forward, the knife feeling more and more like an extension of myself with each attempt.

Shadoe released me from practice, but I tackled him from behind. Taken by surprise, he tried to flip me over his shoulder, but I clung on. Unsuccessfully, he tried again. Finally, my handler crashed into a tree, pinning me between the bark and his body.

He whipped around to face me, my back still pressed against the tree. A flash of anger rippled through his face before he slowly grinned at me. He actually held appreciation in his eyes.

"Better."

I smiled back, but before he could grab me and pummel me, I added, "I want you to teach me how to get through the woods unnoticed."

He gave me a questioning look.

"You're training me how to defend myself and fight, but it's not going to do me much good if I can't sneak up on someone or get away without them tracking me," I announced. "I want you to focus on that too. Not that we can't do the physical training, but I want *stealth* to become a main component of my daily training, too."

While the statement was true enough, I also wanted an excuse to not be constantly beat up the entirety of each training day.

"All right," he said thoughtfully. "I wasn't going to do that until later, but I suppose you're right. Let's go."

Slipping into the woods, we trekked up a small incline. I listened as every branch snapped under my feet, seeming unusually loud. Shadoe, however, was practically unnoticeable.

"Walk on the outsides of your feet," he said, "like this."

I mimicked him and the sound muffled. I must have looked amused because he snickered.

"What else?" I redirected.

"Look for softer earth to step on. If you step on leaves and branches, it's going to make a louder sound."

"You want me to avoid the leaves?" I mocked. "The leaves that cover literally every inch of the earth here? *Those* leaves?"

With that, Shadoe took off ahead of me, silent as a deer. I let out an annoyed huff and followed, trying to catch up. He disappeared from my sight and despite my efforts, I couldn't find him.

"Shadoe?" I asked. *Nothing.*

"Shadoe?" I said again, hoping he would appear and guide us back to camp.

When he didn't reply I gave up. "Fine, I'll figure it out myself."

I swung up into a tree and skittered to the top. I considered looking for him, but decided I didn't care enough. We hadn't gone that far and I could find my way back when I wanted to later; I had come to enjoy my time in the trees, sometimes it was the only peace I had.

I settled myself onto a high branch and watched the world fold out before me. Birds sang as they darted from tree to tree. The leaves tickled my skin as the wind brushed them against me. I could see the smoke from the fires at Lowell's camp.

Closing my eyes, I thought back to my younger years. I could barely remember my parents. I had a few memories to hold on to, but most were fading away. My mother used to take me to a lake and play with me in the shallow water. I remember my father being tall. He had handsome features. I had always seen him as a protector. He would hate to see the vicious way I was learning to fight.

I reached down to arrange my skirt around my knees, only to remember I was in pants that day. Lowell had the women in his group train in both their dresses and pants so that they were prepared to fight either way. The women in his fold were tough. While I preferred the feminine dresses, the pants were easier to train in, especially when I wanted to remain modest while kicking Shadoe in the throat.

"Lur?" I heard a voice say quietly below.

I looked down and saw Shadoe walking toward the tree, having returned to find me, head sweeping from side to side. He didn't know where I was.

"Lur?" he asked again.

I let him walk past me without answering. It was nice to ignore him.

I let him get far enough out of sight before I climbed down. I followed after him, hiding whenever he turned around. As far as I could tell he didn't know I was trailing him. I wished I had thought far enough ahead that I had run back toward the camp and tackled him as he exited the tree line. Of course, I hadn't thought things through.

My mind raced ahead of us, picturing the layout we had traversed earlier. I fought to find a way to gain an advantage. If I took the long way around I could race ahead and catch him. I doubted I would make it.

Staying behind him, I slowly inched closer—step by step—keeping as silent as I could. As Shadoe stepped out of the trees and started toward the camp, I ran as fast as I could. He turned just as my feet left the ground. I collided into his chest and sent us both tumbling to the dirt. The men standing a few yards away burst into laughter as we collapsed.

Shadoe flipped me over onto my back and hovered over me, his eyes wild. He looked as if he wanted to say something; his lips kept twitching, but no words came out. Finally, he let go of my arms and stood up. He walked away without looking back. I couldn't tell if I had won the victory or not.

"...as if he'd never heard her. Isn't that right, Marjorie?" Lowell howled at his own story.

Marjorie sat on his right, giggling at the tale. Annetta, the blonde image of perfection, sat to my right, opposite Lowell. She joined in, encouraging him to continue. Marjorie flipped her short, curly red hair and leaned into Lowell's arm.

My cousin's groupies had joined us for dinner. Every night Lowell had a different parade of women eating with us. I rarely saw him alone. The women cared nothing about me and I had nothing in common with them, so I had become accustomed to dropping my head and staring at my food intently during the course of the meal.

"Auluria," Lowell said jovially, snapping me to attention, "how was training today?"

"It was fine," I said, keeping my words brief, "we worked on knife throwing and stealth training today."

"Good. That's good," he said, almost smiling. I worried about what was in his cup. "Annetta, you're good at being stealthy, aren't you?"

"Yes, Lowell, of course." She giggled back. I saw her reach out with her foot to brush his leg under the makeshift table. She laughed again and Marjorie looked annoyed. "I'm *very* stealthy."

I hated these dinners. I always felt so unwanted. I sighed quietly as I picked at my food.

"Lur," Shadoe said from outside the large tent door. He waved me forward and I looked to Lowell for permission. He nodded and waved me off, so I stood and walked to the door.

I waited for him to give me directions.

"Looked like you needed an excuse to get out of there," Shadoe commented as he turned and walked away.

"Oh," I said, slightly confused. "Thanks."

Unsure of what to do, I followed him. He glanced back, a bit surprised to see me.

"Did you eat?" he asked.

"Not really," I answered.

"Hard with the fans, huh?" Shadoe said knowingly.

"Yeah, they aren't exactly good for the appetite."

"Makes you want to gag, doesn't it?" He almost chuckled.

"Yeah, it kind of does," I agreed. It was nice of him to rescue me.

He led us to a fire on the far side of the camp. Like the day with the water mug, we sat and stared at the fire. I forced some food down, only because I knew I would need my strength for whatever training Shadoe had planned for when we were done. I knew there was no way I'd escape without having to practice, even that late at night.

"Locust!" Shadoe summoned the man over.

"Yeah?" he yelled from across the fire.

Locust, whose real name was not Locust, was slightly older than Shadoe. His brown, floppy hair swept into his face in an interesting way. I had heard he was called Locust because he ate everything in sight.

"I need your help. Come here."

He muttered something unkind and walked over to join us.

"I'm training Lur and I need your help," Shadoe motioned to me still sitting by the fire.

"Well, now that's a different story." His eyebrows shot up and he grinned at me.

"Shut up, Locust. I'm teaching her to pick pocket and I need a dummy," Shadoe said curtly.

"Even better," his grin stretched wider.

Shadoe stooped and picked up a stone from the ground. He handed it to Locust, who showed it to me before putting it in his coat pocket.

"The goal, Lur, is to get the rock out of the pocket without him knowing it."

"What's the point in that?" I interrupted. "We're not thieves."

"No, we're not, but we're not doing it to steal things *just to steal them.* We're doing it in case we ever need to retrieve information from the Society. They write things down and send them with the soldiers all the time. If we can lift that information from them, we have the advantage," Shadoe informed me.

"It's especially important for the pretty girls to know how to do it, because you can usually get so much closer to them without being questioned. In fact, they encourage beautiful women to be near them," Locust said. "Which is, in fact, why I'm not horribly upset to stand here and endure this. Once you get the basics down, you'll be working on the...more *complicated* version." he winked at me.

I frowned. I wasn't sure what he meant.

"Stop it, Locust," Shadoe warned.

"I'm just saying... *You can't do it* because you know what she's doing. You have to be able to watch and correct her form...and *I'm* volunteering to be the test subject again." He elbowed Shadoe happily.

"What are you talking about?" I asked, my voice terse.

"You don't have to do it tonight, and I won't ever make you do it with him," Shadoe assured me.

"Do what, Shadoe?"

He sighed. "The soldiers like pretty girls; they like to be near them. The best way to get close to them is to flirt with them, and usually that leads to kissing them. There's a lot you can accomplish while kissing someone because they are usually so distracted." I knew I looked horrified and Shadoe looked almost as embarrassed as I felt.

"But we're not doing that tonight, so don't worry about it now," he assured me.

It *did* worry me. I didn't want to kiss Locust or anyone in Lowell's fold for that matter. I saw no reason to be kissing at my age. Other girls my age were seeing different boys, but I had never felt the need to while I was so young. I had plenty of time for that.

Shadoe showed me how to use two fingers to reach into the pocket so I was less likely to be noticed. We practiced well into the night, the fire crackling and the stars sparkling. Locust wasn't a bad guy when you got to know him, though I knew I wouldn't be able to put up with him for long periods of time.

By the end of our training session, I had a good grasp on the concept. I was excited to show Lowell the next day.

Chapter 4

"Lowell!" I said, grinning when my cousin walked past me the next morning. "I have something to show you!"

He looked a little upset that I had delayed him from wherever he was going, but he turned around and walked back to me.

I held out my hand, a paper clutched between two fingers. I grinned, waiting for him to catch on.

His eyebrows furrowed, trying to understand. Leaning closer, he realized what the paper was. His hand flew to his pocket and came up empty. He sputtered.

"How?"

I grinned in return, handing him back the paper.

"Huh." He grinned, for the first time looking impressed with me.

"I learned last night."

"Impressive," he confirmed. "I want to see you and Shadoe this morning. Come find me in an hour or so."

I nodded as he walked away.

Walking around the camp, I set out to find Shadoe. Lowell hadn't said it, but I knew it was my job to find him and get him to the meeting on time.

"Well, if it isn't the pickpocket thief that stole my heart," Locust crowed when he saw me approaching.

"Clearly, I took your *rationality* and *sense of self-preservation* as well, Locust," I said as I turned and walked away.

I decided then that I didn't want to be friends with Locust.

It took me twenty minutes, but I finally tracked Shadoe down on the far side of the camp, opposite where he would usually set up his tent. He was smashing his fist into a younger boy's nose. It cracked loudly as I approached. I barely winced, having become familiar with his no-holds method of teaching.

"And that, boys, is how we handle annoyances." A red-haired boy said as I approached. He looked to be about my age; one of Shadoe's former recruits. He laughed as he waved the boys off and took the bleeder to get medical attention.

"Lur," Shadoe addressed me.

"Lowell wants to see us," I said. When he raised his eyebrows in question, I clarified. "I don't know why. I did, however, pick his pocket this morning. He actually seemed impressed."

I grinned. I wanted him to know I had done something right, something *impressive.*

"Good for you," he said just over a mumble. "Come on."

"You wanted to see us?" Shadoe asked as we walked up to Lowell.

We had found him in a meeting with two other men at the far end of the camp. Shadoe waited until the men stepped away before advancing, expecting me to follow behind him.

"Yes. Shadoe, good job with Auluria's training. I can see she's really improving. You two make a very good team," Lowell said as he motioned for us to follow.

We wove a path around the remaining tents and out into the spacious field we found ourselves camping near.

"I think Auluria is ready for her first mission." He threw a glance at Shadoe. "With your oversight, of course. We'll keep it simple at first, but we'll work her up to your level more quickly than the others. I think she can handle it."

I jumped over a small dip in the ground, careful not to twist an ankle before my first mission for Lowell. The tall grass tickled my arms as we walked through it.

"I have decided I like the two of you as a team. You work well together. I think in time, once she is on your level, you will balance each other out," my cousin said, slowing his steps. He stopped and turned to us.

"Shadoe, I want you to look out for Auluria. Yes, you are to train her, but you are also to protect her. There is no one I trust more than the two of you. I know you will work well as a team and you'll be happy together. You make a fine pair, and one day—soon—you both will be my right-hand men. I want you—*together*—to be my second in command."

Lowell kept talking, but I could no longer hear him. *What had he just said? Did he.... Did he really just.... commit me to Shadoe? Did he commit me to Shadoe as more than just a partner... Because it certainly sounded like I was just given to him as the ultimate partner: a bride.*

"You'd like that, wouldn't you, Cousin?" His voice invaded my thoughts again.

"I...what?"

"*Missy*, you will start listening to me when I speak to you, do I make myself clear?" he was annoyed.

"I'm sorry, Lowell, I got a little lost. Did you say you're partnering us together?"

"Of course!" he was restraining himself from shouting. "Haven't you been listening at all?" he rolled his eyes. "Go. Shadoe, go get her ready for the mission. *Honestly*, Auluria, maybe you aren't ready," he spat his words like venom.

I wanted desperately to impress him; to be the leader he wanted me to be. But before I could say anything, Shadoe swept me away, back to the camp to prepare for our mission.

"I'm sorry, Shadoe, that whole partner thing just threw me," I tried to explain.

"It doesn't matter, Lur, how much did you hear?"

"None of the mission details," I admitted sheepishly.

"We're moving; setting up camp elsewhere. Once we arrive and set up, you and I are going on a scouting mission. Nothing too dangerous, but it will be good practice for you," he said. "Go get packed up and we'll talk it over once we arrive."

I sighed and split away from him, walking back to my tent.

I hated having to move. Lowell said it was for the best, but I still didn't like it. It was so much unnecessary work. Most of Lowell's people lived in the towns to avoid suspicion. Some of us moved from site to site to avoid detection. We made regular appearances in the towns, but we never lived in one place for very long.

I gathered my things together, putting my clothing in my bags. We were responsible for our own belongings, so we could take whatever we could carry. I brought several dresses and a few sets of pants and shirts. I had a hairbrush that belonged to my mother with me, and letters from my father. There were a few small trinkets from my childhood I brought along, but I didn't have much to start with.

The tents were taken down and the entire world Lowell created collapsed into bags. We settled into a steady pace, moving to our new temporary home. Shadoe found his way next to me and we walked in silence.

His arm brushed against mine several times on our journey, but I ignored it. I didn't like Lowell telling me what to do, and I imagine Shadoe didn't either, but we'd both do as he said. We were committed to Lowell, and therefore, committed to each other.

I heard him coming before I heard his voice. "Hey,

beautiful," Locust called to me from several yards away. Before he could finish, Shadoe's strong, clear voice cut him off.

"Back off, Locust," he said so low and quiet I almost missed it.

Shadoe's arm slid around my waist under my pack, his hand gripping my arm. I unintentionally stiffened at his touch. Not meaning to, I turned my head to him just in time to see Locust in my peripheral vision. He eyes became incredibly wide and his face flushed white, followed by deep crimson. Locust would no longer be a problem of mine.

Shadoe held his arm around me for a few more yards before he released me, ensuring that people had taken notice. I was claimed. I was Shadoe's. Lowell had proclaimed it so and now Shadoe took ownership of the fact that we were together. I had no choice but to accept it.

When we arrived, Shadoe set his tent up next to mine. The proximity of my trainer was unnerving. I was only starting to get used to him as a mentor, now I had to get used to him as my partner and the man I was committed to. I needed some distance.

"Let's go, Lur," he said as soon as we were both set up.

I wanted to rest; to sit and listen to the crickets, close my eyes and let my mind take me somewhere far away. Instead, I stood and joined him.

He walked closer to me than usual through the camp. Word had already made its way through most of the group just during our journey to the new campsite. Eyes followed us as we walked. Once we were out of eyesight, Shadoe moved away from me, giving me the distance I craved.

"We're going into town." He broke the silence. "One of our spies is there and he needs to pass a message to us. You will be in charge of finding him and procuring the missive. I am there as back up only."

I nodded. My first mission and I was already on my own.

"You know our man; you've seen him before. I will not tell you who he is. You will point him out to me. Then it will be your job to get to him and get the message without anyone noticing. You will run your idea past me first, you may use whatever you need to in order to accomplish the mission. Questions?"

"No, I understand." I started walking faster toward the town and Shadoe kept pace.

"Good. It's busy; it's the middle of the day. That should help with your cover. But don't get caught," he warned.

I wished I knew the layout of the town. If I knew in advance what I was working with, I could have formulated a plan while we walked. Instead, I had wait until we approached to finalize my thoughts.

I searched the crowd for our mark. We were perched up on a hill, lying in the grass, looking down at the market. Business was being held on the outskirts of the town, clearly a good place for our kind of people to gather. It had the advantage of easy exits; a person could run to the woods, through the town, or hide in a nearby house or store if needed. There was a clear sightline to the main roads both *in* the town and *entering* the town. If the Society showed up, they would know and be able to escape.

Men wandered everywhere. Women hastened children along. I could hear the hum of conversation even from on the hill. My eyes swept the crowd again, looking for anything familiar.

I pointed to a man in dark clothing. His beard hid most of his face, and what wasn't hidden was covered by a low-pulled hat. When Shadoe nodded my heart jumped. *I can do this.*

Now I needed a plan. I glanced around, calculating

my next move. Merchants were selling goods. Men were trying to haggle for better prices. A fight broke out and we could hear the shouting.

I stood to run, seeing my opportunity. Shadoe pulled me back. "I have to go, now!" I hissed.

He pressed something cold and metallic into my hand. A knife. I took it and slipped it into my boot, not telling him I already had knives safely tucked away in both my boot and belt.

I slipped over the grass and looped around the back of the group. No one noticed me come up behind them. Most were turned to make sure they stayed out of the range of the fight.

Walking up to a merchant who was selling bags and pouches, I leaned against his makeshift stand, admiring his creations. I ran my fingers across the smooth fabrics and leathers of the bags.

"You like?" he asked.

I gave him a small smile, "Yes, they're very nice."

I ran my fingers across them again, examining each one. I saw my contact approach the stand next to the one I was at, only a few feet away.

"I'm looking for something I can attach to my belt at the hip," I said, "This one isn't very effective." I pointed to the small bag I was carrying.

When Shadoe had handed me the knife, I balanced myself on his arm as I slipped it into my boot. I forced myself to stumble into him as I righted myself, and I stole his money pouch. I kept it hidden in front of me as I ran.

I picked up a bag and let it dangle in my fingers. Holding it to my hip, I tried it on for size. Amazingly, it fit perfectly, especially since I hadn't planned it.

"This one, I think." I held it up to the light once more, admiring the detail work.

He named a price; too high. I bartered; he bartered back. Once we finally reached an agreement, I set the bag on the very edge of the stand, next to my contact.

Opening Shadoe's pouch, I intentionally spilled part of the contents.

"Oh," I gasped and reached forward to scoop it up. The man reached forward to help me; I saw my contact slip the letter into the bag I had just set down. I picked it up as the bag-maker scooped up the last of my coins, counting them out for me. With pouch clutched firmly in my hand, I pulled a few extra coins out to make up the difference of what the merchant had in his hand.

I felt the thick paper in the pouch, but was careful not to crinkle it. I thanked the man and turned to walk away. My contact stayed at his table, still waiting for his turn to be served. I was grateful it had been a busy booth, selling food to the men and women of the town.

I weaved my way around merchants and people. Attaching my new pouch to my belt, I felt strangely exhilarated. I stopped at several stands, examining the goods I had no intention of buying. I didn't want to make myself noticed by appearing at one stand and then disappearing.

A hand reached around me and snaked its way to the pouch on my belt. I had my knife against his wrist before I realized it was Shadoe testing me. I removed it, but not before lightly scraping it across his skin, causing blood to bubble up. I smiled to myself.

"Let's go," he said, wiping the blood away and moving fully to my side. In his hand, he clutched a few supplies he must have attained while watching me.

"How did you get those?" I asked, realizing I had taken his money.

"I carry money in more than one place, Lur, I didn't steal these." He sounded offended.

"Well, how was I to know?" I shot back.

"I see you brought your own knife," he commented.

"Two, actually," I corrected.

"You're learning," We started back up the hill. "Let me have the letter." He reached out his hand, waiting for me to hand it to him, a wise choice, considering I would have sliced his hand again if he had tried to take it.

"No, I think I'll carry it back to Lowell," I said, "It is my first mission, after all, and I want to see it through."

"This is going to be a fun partnership, isn't it?" he sounded annoyed again.

"Apparently," I agreed.

Chapter 5

Lowell kicked me out immediately, opting to talk only to Shadoe. When I was finally allowed back in, two more of Lowell's groupies were sitting at the table, fawning over him. It made me sick the way his women threw themselves at him. At least I'd never have to do that with Shadoe.

"You're going back out," Lowell said jovially as the women laughed. "Eat quickly, then go."

"No, we'll eat on the way," Shadoe said, grabbing my arm and spinning me out of the room.

"You don't want to stay there," he whispered as we walked away from Lowell's large tent.

The truth was, I never liked being around Lowell

when he had women around. If Shadoe spared me another wasted night with my cousin sitting in silence with my head hanging down, then I was grateful to him.

Weaving our way around the tents, we picked up food from his friends as we moved past them. We ate as we walked and I let him guide me to our next mission.

"Where are we going, Shadoe?"

"There has been some unrest near the town. We need to go see what's been happening," he said.

I hesitated once we reached the woods. Shadoe had said we were going to gather information on the unrest near the town, he had never said we were going into the woods.

It wasn't that I feared the woods. I liked the woods, especially when everything was so calm and peaceful. But something immediately didn't feel right as we stepped through the tree line.

A branch cracked to my left and I stopped. Shadoe kept walking, but I knew he had to have heard it. Suddenly they were everywhere. Screams filled the night as footsteps raced toward me.

I saw Shadoe fall to the ground in front of me, a boy collapsed on top of him. Arms wrap around me in a collision of great speed. I flipped him over me, knowing it was coming before he even touched me. More noise clouded the air.

"Shadoe!" I screamed, hoping for an answer.

"I'm here Lur," he yelled back. I could see him grappling with someone on the ground.

I could hear flesh striking flesh as I struggled against the attack. Someone grunted but I couldn't tell if it was Shadoe or one of the other men. My face snapped back as a fist hit me, sending searing pain throughout my jaw.

I turned and lashed out at my attacker. He yelped in pain as I connected. I guessed there were five or six men who had ambushed us. Someone grabbed me around the waist from behind and lifted me into the air.

"Settle down," he commanded as I kicked in the air.

The voice. I recognized it. It was one of Shadoe's men. It wasn't an ambush...*it was a test.*

I wrapped my foot around the back of his ankle and kicked it out, sending us both toppling to the ground. I pushed him off of me, spinning on my knee. I regretted it instantly as twigs drove their way into my kneecap. Swinging my other leg over him, I pinned him to the ground and I started in on his face.

Another man pulled me away several punches later. I jerked my head back, crashing into his jaw causing him to stumble and release me. I slammed the heel of my hand into his nose and heard it crack. He cursed as I shoved his shoulders, sending him to the ground.

The man reached for my ankle and I fell. A foot embedded itself in my side. Groaning, I pulled myself upright. I lashed my hand out at the man, clawing his face.

I ran toward the man pinning Shadoe down. Now that I knew that he wasn't actually being attacked, I considered letting him stay there. I hoped the man had time to get a few good punches in before I tackled him. On the ground, I kicked the man in the stomach and he doubled over. I took the opportunity to bring my boot up and kick him in the groin, ensuring he would stay on the ground.

Shadoe had "taken out" the other two men, so I turned my fury on Shadoe. He was just standing up as I pushed him backwards. I shoved him again, and then one more time for good measure. My hand reeled back, winding up to slap him when he reached out and grabbed my hand to stop me.

"Lur!" he warned.

I took the opportunity to turn away from him, twisting out of his grasp, as I brought my boot down hard on his foot.

"Ow! *Lur!*"

"What is the *matter* with you?" I yelled. "You had your men attack me? What was the point in that?" I shouted.

"If you wanted me to train against them, all you had to do was pair me with them! You didn't need to drag me out to the woods in the dark of night and have them attack me!" My voice grew louder. "I *hope* they got some good punches in, because if *they* didn't mess up your face, *I will!*"

I was enraged. My face throbbed. My side hurt where I had been kicked and I knew there would be a massive bruise in the morning. I felt like I had been shattered.

"*Auluria, stop!*" he commanded, the spark in his eyes dulling.

I froze and retracted my hand. I couldn't steady my breathing though. Then I realized the piece I had been missing.

"Lowell knew," I said quietly. "He sent me out here for this."

"Yes," Shadoe said quietly, stepping toward me. "He knew." He turned and dismissed the others, leaving us alone.

"It's a rite of passage, Lur. Everyone involved in missions goes through a jumping. We have to make sure you can handle yourself if something goes sideways on a mission. We need to know you could take care of your-self if something happens to your partner."

"*Well I think we've established I can,*" I said spitefully, cradling my dominant hand, covered in fresh blood.

He reached for my shoulder but I pulled away. I started walking back to the camp, Shadoe trailing behind me. I refused to listen to him so he finally gave up trying to explain. We settled into our cold, common, silence.

I crashed into Lowell's tent, the two girls still hanging on him.

"You knew!" I screeched. I didn't care. "You knew and you sent me anyway! You didn't even warn me."

"You weren't supposed to know, Auluria," he slurred. "That's the whole point."

I wanted to slap him. I wanted to knock him to the ground and spit at him. Instead I stood, seething, before him. My chest rose and fell so deeply I could feel my entire body move with it.

Lowell's demeanor shifted and the girls backed away. Slipping out of the tent behind Lowell, they left us to our conversation.

"You listen to me, *Missy*," he said between gritted teeth. "This is the way things are here. You *will* comply."

He was angry even in his inebriated state.

"We had to make sure you could handle yourself and you proved you could… At least, I assume you did. " He looked me up and down before continuing. "And you did it a heck of a lot faster than most people do it. That's why I'm trusting you to be my second in command and to be with Shadoe."

He seemed to calm a bit. "*You*, Cousin, are the key to our success. You know that. Just do as I say and the time will come for you to take your rightful place as my Second with Shadoe soon."

He looked ready to pass out. Suddenly my anger dimmed, though it didn't extinguish. I caught his hand and guided him to a seat. My side was pierced with pain and my breath caught as I lowered him.

"And what if I just want a normal life, Lowell?" I asked quietly, knowing he'd never remember in the morning.

"Oh, but dear Cousin, you were meant for so much more." He gave me a half smile, as his eyes rolled back and closed.

"You were meant to champion the fight and help bring us to glory…" His voice trailed off.

I left him hanging out of the chair.

Stepping into my tent, I sunk onto my mattress. I pulled the blankets around me, not bothering to change. Everything hurt. My head ached. I just wanted peace.

"Lur?"

"Go away, Shadoe," I said angrily.

"Can I come in?" he asked.

I threw a pillow at the entrance. Without turning to see my aim, I heard it hit before sliding to the ground. Shadoe stepped in anyway.

"Get out!" I shouted.

"I have to make sure you're okay first," he responded, walking to my side.

I thought about hitting him, but it required too much energy. I just wanted to stop for the day.

"Let me see," he insisted.

"Leave me alone, Shadoe. I don't need you and I certainly don't want you," I said, viciousness lacing my voice.

It was hard to see in the small tent, but in the moonlight filtering through the fabric of the tent, I was positive I saw him pull back slightly.

"Martin said he kicked you. Just let me check it." He reached for me and I didn't stop him. "You know it wasn't my choice, right?" he muttered softly while he examined my side.

"Of course it was," I snapped back, louder than I meant to. "You always have a choice, Shadoe. Always."

"Lowell said–"

"I don't care what Lowell said. *You* are my mentor. You're *supposed* to be my partner, and from what I can tell, *my fiancé. You're* supposed to look out for me. I should come first, before Lowell or any of his stupid mandates. You knew I was ready, so there was no need for that," I huffed. "I can't believe I was actually worried for you. When they attacked, I genuinely thought they had hurt you and I was terrified you were going to get hurt worse."

I heard him breathe in sharply, though whether it was directed at my words or my injuries, I didn't know.

"One thing is for sure, I'll never worry about you again," I spat. "You're on your own, I don't care what Lowell says. If I have to see you every day for the rest of our lives, so be it, but I won't lose any sleep over you getting hurt."

"Lur, stop talking," he said quietly. "I need to see this."

He wanted me to stop and I didn't care. This place, these people… They had destroyed any softness I once had long ago, when I first came to this group. All that was left was a fighter. They had trained me and molded me and I was exactly what they wanted: a soldier devoid of free will—or maybe the will to care.

He finished checking my injuries and left. The dark was welcoming. I watched the moonlight cast shadows through my tent. I wanted to crawl out and see the stars, but I hurt too much to move. I finally drifted off to sleep.

Chapter 6

A month later, I had finally given up on despising Shadoe. I had long since forgiven Lowell, my only remaining family. Shadoe and I worked together; each day I became a little less cold toward him.

Eventually, we returned to our comfortable silence. We carried out our assignments, learned to read each other's signals, and we fell into a comfortable working partnership.

"Go around," he whispered to me as we walked into the town.

I nodded and split off. I slipped around to the backside of the group, Shadoe wandering in from the front.

The mission was simple enough: retrieve weapons from a Society stockpile. We would be breaking into a makeshift building and taking as much as we could. *Our* job was to break in and open it up to the other team members who would follow.

The sun had set and people were wandering back to their homes for the evening. Soon our team would be cloaked in darkness and could easily sneak in.

I wandered toward the building, avoiding the people walking toward me. I kept my eyes down, refusing to make eye contact. My hand brushed over the pouch on my hip, my knife resting under it, hidden from sight.

Shadoe approached the building first and slipped into the shadows along its side. The streets quieted as I joined him. We sunk into the depths of the darkness and waited. Once it was silent, Shadoe checked to make sure we really were alone.

He blocked me from view as I broke the lock on the makeshift building. If we were caught, it would be easier for *him* to explain away why he was out so late. It would not be nearly as easy for me, a woman, to explain why I was out alone so late at night.

Within moments I had the door open and we slipped in together. It would be a bit before the rest of the team arrived. We examined the boxes and bags sitting in the room.

"Here," Shadoe said, handing me something. "Eat, there's time."

I bit into the apple, grateful for the sweet taste. It had been a long time since I had been able to enjoy my food. Usually I was rushing to eat so I could get to my training or a mission. It tasted like relief.

"They'll be here soon," he stated after a few minutes.

"We should decide what we need," I added.

We rifled through the contents of the makeshift building. Shadoe and I started shifting knives and weapons under our clothing. Within minutes the team arrived and started doing the same.

Shadoe and I positioned ourselves outside the building and acted as lookouts, having already taken on our loads to transport. My eyes adjusted to the dark outside that was only slightly brighter than the inside of the building because of the stars and uninhibited moon.

I crept around to the back of the building and waited. The crickets chirped lazily nearby as I settled into my watch post. Everything seemed so still. I tried to keep my mind from wandering, focusing intently on the landscape before me.

It wasn't until I heard the crickets drop off one by one that I started to worry. I could sense danger coming. Taking a deep breath, I edged my way back to the front of the makeshift building.

Shadoe saw me clinging to the side of the building as I

entered into the space he was monitoring. He turned and signaled into the building. The team started moving quickly toward us, having nearly reached the door at the same time as I did.

"Halt!" The voice nearly made me jump.

Shadoe and I froze. The man stood closest to me, his men behind him. I slowly turned and straightened. Facing him, I caught sight of his government uniform: Society.

"What are you doing?" He addressed me.

I waited for Shadoe's signal but it never came. I moved so quickly the man never expected it. The blow to his face sent him careening backward into two of his men. They all stumbled, one falling to the ground entirely.

I didn't wait. I launched myself at another man and Shadoe followed suit. The people poured out from the building, some helping us in the brawl, others keeping the stolen supplies safe by running.

Pain radiated through my shoulder as a soldier pulled my arm behind me. "Don't move," he ordered.

I heard a snap and the pressure released. The man lay on the ground behind me, Shadoe standing over him; he snapped the soldier's neck.

"You okay?" he asked. I nodded and he turned to hold back another man's punch, crushing a bone in his wrist.

I started to help one of the team members when a pair of arms wrapped tightly around my waist.

"Look here boys, we have a girl!" the soldier shouted.

"Hang on to her—they'll want her at the camps," another replied.

The thought of the camps terrified me. If a young person was caught alone, they tended to disappear. Boys were sent to training camps to learn to fight against the foreign countries that wanted to invade. Girls were sent to breeding camps to boost the population count. I didn't know which was worse. Orphans were always the first to be taken, but if they found you isolated, they'd take you too. I'd even heard rumors about them taking older women when they could. The government would do anything to avoid attack.

As he mentioned the camps I could feel myself panic. Everything in me stiffened. I knew I had to get out of his grasp. I clawed at his hands and arms, but he only laughed.

"This one's a fighter."

"Strong willed, huh?" his friend retorted.

He moved over next to us and ran his hands through my hair, brushing it away from my face. "Pretty, too. I bet we could get a pretty penny for this one—"

Before he could finish, I bit him. It was so hard I drew blood. He scowled and backed away.

The first man wrenched me away from the soldier I

just bit. Kneeing the back of my legs, he sent me sprawling to the ground. He collapsed on top of me so I could not escape. His legs straddled either side of me, pinning me to the ground in a kneeling position.

Throwing my head back, I collided with his nose and jaw and the man let out a shriek of pain.

"Get away from me!" I yelped, trying to get free.

His hand clawed at my shoulder, trying desperately to hold me in place. I was grateful to be wearing pants during the mission; had I been in a dress, I would have tangled myself up in it trying to free myself of his hold. I threw my elbow back at him, hitting him in the face again. This time he let go.

I felt Shadoe's hand grab mine and pull me the rest of the way to my feet.

"Go," he ordered and I obeyed. I heard the man take his last breath as Shadoe finished him off. A moment later my partner was at my side.

We rallied in the woods. We had escaped with only a few minor injuries, most of the damage being done to the Society soldiers.

"You okay?" Shadoe asked, glancing at me for only a moment to make sure I had no life-threatening injuries.

"I'm fine," I brushed the dirt off of myself as we waited for the last of our team to trickle in. "You?"

"Fine," he said.

"Lowell's not going to be happy we got caught

tonight," I commented.

"No, but at least we all got away."

"And we got most of what we went for," I added with a shrug.

The camp was quiet when we entered. Shadoe and I found Lowell in his tent, going over some papers in his hands.

"Well?" he asked without looking up.

"We ran into some trouble with some soldiers, but we all made it back."

Lowell's gaze shot up for a moment, burning into Shadoe. Then he relaxed and turned back to his papers. "And you got everything?"

"Yes," Shadoe confirmed.

"Good," he nodded. "Tomorrow you and Auluria need to go to town. One of our men will be delivering a message to us."

"And you can't send someone less over qualified?" I mutter.

His head whipped up when he heard me and I immediately backed down.

"I would like for you and Shadoe to handle this, *Missy*."

"Of course, Lowell. Whatever you need," I said softly.

He dismissed us and we made our way back to our tents.

"Well, that turned out well," I muttered and Shadoe

shot me a withering look. It didn't matter how Lowell spoke to us, Shadoe would always take his side.

Without commenting further, I slipped into my tent.

The town was crowded the next morning. We were on high alert because there was a good chance the soldiers were looking for us after the events of the previous night.

I was operating on minimal sleep, but the bright sun was enough to keep me focused as it blinded me from above. Shadoe and I split apart and made our way down into the throngs of people.

I tried to blend in as I wove my way around the streets. Our spy would be meeting with Shadoe, I was merely there for distraction or back up if necessary. I watched as he moved ahead of me, making his way to our contact.

I stopped to examine some food that different vendors were selling in the streets, turning my attention completely away from my partner. My ears were sharply focused in for the sound of his voice, even if I wasn't watching him with my eyes.

"Looks good, doesn't it, miss?" A man's voice caught my attention.

I met his gaze and found him holding something out to me to examine.

"Yes, it looks wonderful," I said. "I'm not sure what I want though."

"We have a wonderful assortment of breads. Would you like to try one?" he tempted me, holding out a small piece he ripped off of a loaf.

I reached out to take it, savoring the crispness of it.

I heard a commotion over my shoulder and turned to look. Shadoe was slowly backing away from his contact, trying to blend with the crowd. His contact was standing in the middle of a large group, yelling.

Another man, he looked to be a vendor, was shouting at him, accusing him of something. Shadoe stared at me until he could tell I had turned my gaze on him and he motioned for us to get out.

I thanked the man, but declined his offer. Turning I tried to slip away, only to find myself confronted by a wall of people. They gathered around to watch the fight, blocking my escape. I ducked back the way I had come and tried to make my way around the vendors to a side street.

When I caught sight of Shadoe again, he was making his escape hastily away from the crowd. He never saw the man step toward him, readying his knife.

Before I could call out, a second man joined the first. As I began to panic, I saw the second man carefully stick out his leg, catching the first man's foot, causing him to stumble, as if it were all an accident.

The second man bent down, catching the first man's arm before he hit the ground. Apologizing profusely, he helped dust the man off, pocketing the knife he had dropped during the fall. The first man swatted at him and cursed. He looked around for his knife as the second man slipped into the crowd and hid from view.

The man who saved Shadoe glanced up just in time to catch my gaze. He shot me a brilliant grin that lit up his blue eyes. His eyebrows moved up in a yeah-I-just-saved-that-guy way, tousling his dark hair. Before I could move, he was gone again, slipping through the crowd.

He had no idea who Shadoe was or what he was doing, but he saved him anyway, even knowing it could have caused his own stabbing. I was surprised by his actions, but didn't have time to question it.

The first man came back into my view, and I realized he was wearing a Society uniform. He must have seen the exchange, or at least suspected. He was off duty, so his uniform was minimal, but could still be identified as one of them.

I ran to meet Shadoe, concerned that the first man might come back to look for him. When I caught up to him, he confirmed he had the message we had been there to transfer, but had no idea how the man had spotted him. It didn't matter though; we needed to move.

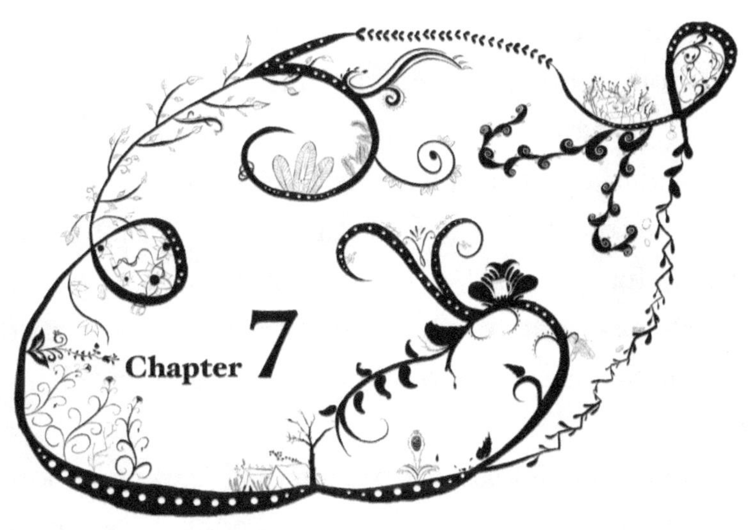

Chapter 7

"This is good," Lowell says, studying the papers. He looked up at us and added, "You both did very well. This is information regarding the master plan. It was incredibly important we got this information. Well done."

Shadoe nodded, but I could tell he was proud to have accomplished something so important for Lowell. I was still worried about almost being caught.

"You both need to start taking on more responsibility," Lowell continued. "Auluria, I think this is the perfect time for you to plan our next mission. What do you think, Shadoe?"

"I think she'll do fine, Lowell." He nodded, hands behind his back like the perfect soldier.

"Good, good. We're moving in three days. Once we get to the new town, we'll need to do some scouting. Have Auluria prepare a team; let's see how she does."

I spent the next two days putting together a team and formulating a plan. I decided everything from the rendezvous point to what time we would leave on the mission. Shadoe oversaw and only offered a few changes to my plan.

I took a small team for the mission. It went smoothly and we were not noticed. I was proud of myself as I delivered the information to Lowell. He was almost as proud.

"You haven't been with us long, Auluria, but already you have proven yourself to be one of our greatest achievements. I no longer see the need to oversee you. Your training is complete. Now you can take your place in the ranks," my cousin said as we walked.

"Shadoe will still be your partner, but no longer your mentor. You'll work together as a team."

"I understand," I confirm, lifting my skirt as I stepped over a fallen tree branch.

"The pieces are falling together, Auluria. For now, focus on the missions I give you, but know: your day is coming. When it draws near, we'll give you some more specific training you will need for the mission, but that won't be until you are a bit older."

Time passed quickly and slowly all at once. A year later Shadoe and I quickly became regarded as Lowell's right-hand man and his highly esteemed, *female*, cousin.

More time passed and the people started looking to Shadoe for leadership almost as much as they did to Lowell. Lowell stepped further and further back, letting Shadoe take on more responsibility. He was training Shadoe to take over for him, if the time ever came.

Later, when I was seventeen, Lowell came to find me one late afternoon with something on his mind, ready to move forward with his plan.

"Auluria, I think it's time we add a few new skills to your training," Lowell said as we walked around the camp.

"All right," I said cautiously.

"I'd like you to spend some time with a woman I know from town."

My heart dropped to my stomach. I never liked the women Lowell knew, and I imagined this one would be no exception.

"Tomorrow morning, you'll go to her and spend a few days with her. She'll have a bed waiting for you there."

My heart jumped at the thought of a real bed to sleep in. It had been so long since the days when I lived in my aunt's house. The bed was small and lumpy, but it was better than sleeping on the ground.

"I'll take you there myself in the morning. I want to check in on her anyway. Shadoe will pick you up before we move on."

I thought about pressing for more information, but I knew that would just result in a lecture, so I kept quiet.

"I need you to do whatever she tells you to do, Auluria. She knows what she is talking about."

I nodded to let him know I was listening, though my mind was already spinning off in different directions, trying to figure out what lessons she would be teaching me.

The next day I found Shadoe waiting outside my tent.

"You're leaving?" he asked.

"Lowell didn't tell you?"

"No." He shook his head as my cousin approached us.

"Where is she going, Lowell?" Shadoe confronted him gently.

"I'm sending her to training. I figured it was better coming from Brittella than from you." He smirked, making me uneasy.

The look in Shadoe's eyes did nothing to alleviate that fear.

"She's going to see Brittella?"

"Would you rather we let Locust teach her?"

"No," Shadoe said far too quickly.

"What exactly does this Brittella teach?" I interjected.

"Come along and you'll find out," Lowell said as he started to walk away.

I try catching Shadoe's eye but he refused to look at me.

"I'll come get you in a few days, Lur," Shadoe said before turning and sauntering off.

I rushed after Lowell to catch up, my bag over my shoulder. A gentleman might have offered to carry my pack, but Lowell was a leader and did no such thing.

Toward the edge of town, Lowell walked up to a door and knocked. After a moment, the door swung open and I found a woman fifteen years older than Lowell staring back at us.

"Lowell, come in," she greeted us warmly, her voice low and soothing.

Her dark hair was swept back, leaving part of it cascading over her back; the other half was woven in intricate patterns on her head. Her dress was slightly fancier than mine, enough to show she was of higher standing, but not enough to draw attention from the soldiers.

"Who have you brought me?" she asks, slipping her arm into Lowell's.

She was unlike the girls that followed Lowell around. Rather than hang on him, she allowed him to fuss over *her*, using her touch to illicit responses from him. She guided him to the kitchen, leaving me in the doorway. I waited as they talked for a few moments before Lowell stood up from his seat at her table.

"Listen to her, Auluria, and don't give her any trouble," he pointed at me.

He walked to the door, but was stopped by the sound of Brittella clearing her throat. She stood in the entryway and waited as he made his way back to her, quickly moving her against the wall. He fell into her arms faster than I had ever seen him move with any of the girls that followed him around.

Her movements demanded that she be kissed, and he obeyed submissively. She pushed him back and sent him on his way. I could tell he hadn't had his fill of time with her, but she was clear in her motions and sent him away.

When she turned back to me, I realized why I was there. She was to teach me the art of manipulating a man.

My eyes must have grown fiercely wide, because she grinned at me.

"Don't worry, child. You won't have to do anything you aren't comfortable with," she assured me. "You must be hungry. Come, let's get to know each other."

She led me back to the table where Lowell had just been seated at. Setting food before me, we stared at each other.

"So, Auluria, Lowell tells me you are engaged to a young man. You must be excited."

"It was Lowell's idea," I muttered.

She laughed in response.

"Well, perhaps we'll get you a little more excited about the idea of marrying him by the time we're through. Is he a good lover?"

"I...I..." I was shocked.

"You've never kissed him then, I take it."

"No." I shook my head quickly.

"Well, my dear, at some point you will have to, and it's best to learn the right way to do so. I'll tell you all about that. But more than that, you will be learning how to manipulate and coerce men into doing what you want them to do. Even more than that, you can use these methods to manipulate anyone into doing anything for you." She grinned. "How do you think I got Lowell, a man fifteen years younger than me and constantly surrounded by beautiful women, to think so fondly of me?"

I swallowed.

"I promise, it's not as scary as it sounds." She sat back and gazed kindly at me.

We spent the next three days running over techniques of flirtation and manipulation. I learned to sway when I walked. She showed me how to touch a person's arms to get them to relax and trust me. Brittella taught me how to be unassuming, gentle and graceful so that no one would suspect I was manipulating them. I learned how to captivate attention simply from the way I walked, moved my hair, batted my eyelashes or spoke.

I learned all the right words to say. She brought in people to test me and made me comfortable with being around people. By the time Shadoe arrived to pick me up before the fold left, she decided I was ready.

"So, this is your young man coming to pick you up then?" she asked as we sat on her couch.

"It should be Shadoe, yes."

"You should practice on him," she said, her eyes glittering. "I don't have to watch if you don't like."

My worry had faded away over the three days and I became comfortable with her presence, but what she was suggesting disturbed me. I had no intention of kissing Shadoe to prove a point, much less trying any of the other skills she had begged me to learn despite my refusal.

"I will do no such thing."

"All right, all right. At least try touching his arm a bit.

See how he responds. It doesn't have to be here, but perhaps later today or tomorrow. When he's not expecting it. It might just get you both to warm up to each other." She laughed again, the idea of young love filling her manipulative mind.

"Brittella, I really don't see that happening," I said, to which she only rolled her eyes.

"At least I've taught you," the woman said. "What you do now is up to you. You are ready for whatever Lowell's plan is. Even the parts you wouldn't try, you've been given enough information to figure it out as you go if you need to."

She smiled again. "You'll do splendidly, Auluria. I know you will."

The knock on the door cut her off and she rose and swayed her way over to her door. Opening it, Shadoe stepped into view, appearing more nervous than usual.

"I'm here for Auluria," he said.

"Yes, I know." Brittella appraised him, looking him up and down. "Come in," she added seductively and I saw Shadoe swallow.

"Time to go," he said, locking eyes with me.

I picked up my bag and followed him out to the street. I turned to thank Brittella but she was already gone, having beckoned a handsome man into her door.

We didn't talk at first. I could sense we were both embarrassed by the situation.

"Did I miss anything while I was at training?" I asked, wanting to break the silence.

"Not really," Shadoe replied. "The rest of them already left, so we're catching up with them now. We should meet up with them soon."

"That's good," I said, searching for something else to say. When I found nothing, we fell back into silence.

"How did your training go?" Lowell asked when he saw we had joined the group.

"Britella was… *informative*," I supplied, unsure of what to say.

I saw Locust look in my direction when he realized we were talking. Word must have made its way around that I was being trained by Brittella. I tore my gaze away from the hungry look in his eyes. I still didn't like the man.

"Good," Lowell replied. "Tomorrow we're going to put that to the test."

Before I could speak, Lowell cut me off. "We need you to distract a man tomorrow. You can do it however you see fit. Shadoe is going to be stealing something from his store and you need to assist him."

I couldn't object so I simply nodded.

I thought Shadoe might say something to me, but he didn't. He remained as cool toward me as always. I suppose I was glad he hadn't changed over this.

Chapter 8

I leaned in toward the man, gently placing my hand on his arm as I gazed down at the tray he was holding. He inclined his head, studying me as I looked at the metal pieces on the tray.

Taking my hand off of his arm, I moved the tip of my shoulder to his arm, and brushed my fingertips over the contents of the tray while I murmured questions to him.

He answered every one, never taking his eyes off of me. I could sense Shadoe slip behind us and into a back room. Moments later, he returned and walked to the door. Once he was outside, I began to pout that the pieces were too much for me.

The man tried to negotiate, but I continued to pout. He couldn't part with the pieces without selling them, but he offered bits of scraps that he had turned into a neck-lace for me. I pocketed it and slipped out the door. His eyes didn't leave me until I was out of sight.

"Did you get it?" I asked, dropping the act the moment I had rounded the corner.

Shadoe held up several items for me to inspect.

"What is it?" I asked.

"Here, look," he said, handing me several of the pieces, but keeping one in his hand. He slipped his fingers through it and the piece sat on his knuckles, a harsh and merciless weapon.

"It's like claws," I gasped.

"It's more than that, Lur," he grinned at me but refused to further elaborate.

"What's it for?" I asked.

"Certain missions. Don't worry about it," he said, depositing them in his pack as we walked back to camp.

"Shadoe, do we know what Lowell's big plan is yet? He hasn't told me, but has he talked to you about it?"

"Yes, Lur. I know some of the details, but it's up to Lowell to tell you himself."

"Am I really that important to this plan?" I asked, annoyed.

"Yes, Lur, you really are."

I couldn't imagine how that could be possible if I hadn't even been given any details yet.

"What happens after we finish the plan? How are we

going to change the Society? Does Lowell have a plan for that too?" I questioned.

"Yes, Lur. He has a plan. Haven't you realized by now that your cousin has *everything* figured out?"

"I suppose. I just wish he wouldn't leave me in the dark."

"Then talk to him about it."

His insistence on always deferring to Lowell was starting to bother me. It was as if we couldn't even have a conversation as partners without him referring to our leader.

"I should have stayed at Britella's" I muttered under my breath. "At least she talked to me like a person."

"What?" Shadoe asked, knowing I was complaining about something.

"Nothing. Let's get back."

Each week brought more missions, always with Shadoe by my side. We refrained from talking most of the time, but we worked well together. We had learned each other's moves and knew what the other would do. We made an exceptional team that could anticipate everything before it happened.

Early one afternoon, Shadoe and I walked back to

camp after planting a communication in one of the towns. I tripped in a covered hole and twisted my ankle. Shadoe bent down to check it, placing me against a tree for balance.

When he stood back up, he assured me it would be fine. Without warning, he stepped closer to me. He placed his hand on my hip and leaned in toward me, brushing his lips against mine. I was so surprised I couldn't move.

He pulled back to look at me. Without a word, he leaned in once more, kissing my lips again. I stood frozen against the tree as he walked off.

I should have known it had to come eventually, but I had always thought my first kiss would be…more.

There was nothing I could do, so I followed after him. Neither of us spoke about it.

Two weeks later, we were swimming in a pond, working to keep our stamina up to training standards, when I found myself face to face with Shadoe again.

His arm found its way around my waist and he held me to him as he kissed me. This kiss was longer, but shared the same lack of passion. I kissed him back, trying to please him, knowing he was the only man I'd ever be with and I should make the effort to make it work. He pulled back and swam away.

My heart sank. I was bound to Shadoe. I'd be married

to him one day. This was the man I would be with. He wasn't what I had imagined for myself, but I accepted it.

At least he made the effort. In public, he showed little care for me, in private he barely showed more. But this was a start. Perhaps one day we could grow to care for each other. I had no choice, so, I, at least, would try. If he wanted to kiss, I would kiss him. It was the best effort I could make.

Our next kiss was a few weeks later. We found ourselves in a fight with an opposing group out in the woods. Shadoe and I were attacked first and I suffered a few serious injuries.

Once we fought off our attackers, Shadoe brought me back to my tent and laid me down. He inspected my injuries and for the first time I saw genuine worry on his face.

Without telling me what was wrong, he leaned over me and buried his lips against mine. His hand grazed my hip and I recoiled in pain. His lips didn't leave mine as he kissed me again. He pulled back a moment later, his hand flitting over my hair.

"I'm sorry," he whispered and rushed out of my tent.

I looked down to examine my own injuries. A few days later, I was walking around camp as if nothing too tragic had happened, my injuries having quickly started to heal.

"How are you feeling?" Lowell asked a few days later.

"I'm fine, Lowell. Do you need me for something?"

"Yes, actually." He waved me over. "Take a look here. I need you to familiarize yourself with this, can you do that?"

I looked over the paper in front of him and nodded.

"What are these?" I asked, "Is this… information on people?"

"Yes, Cousin, that's exactly what it is. This is for your next mission. I want to make sure you can learn about these people and then use the information to handle a mission. This is our last big step before the master plan is put into play."

"You have a few hours to look these over. Be back here this afternoon."

Walking away, I looked over the writing. My target appeared to be a man and a woman from the town near where we were camping. I followed along with the words that were written on the pages, committing each notation to memory. When I felt prepared, I found Lowell early.

"I'm ready," I announced.

"Good, let's go."

He walked me toward the town. Silence stretched between us.

"Do well with this, Auluria," he finally said "and we will be ready to move forward; it won't be long now."

"What exactly am I supposed to do once I find these people?"

"Get into their home. You can find your way in. Once you are there, gain their trust, then find a way to be alone and locate the lock that fits this key and retrieve whatever is inside."

I reached out and took the key from him, slipping it into my boot alongside my knife. He pointed out a small home in the middle of the town and sent me on my way.

Walking by myself was a relief. It had been such a long time since I was alone with my thoughts, perhaps even years. I had time alone in my tent every night, but being surrounded by Lowell's people did nothing to give me the solitude I craved.

Shifting my knife and the key away from my boot and into my belt, I watched the house for a few minutes. When I was sure the woman could see me, I loudly walked by her house, throwing myself to the ground with a sharp cry.

I allowed the tears to spring to my eyes, though my deceitful injury caused me no real pain. The bruising I sustained from the attack days before was enough to make the woman cringe. She forced her husband to carry me into their home.

She rushed about her house, gathering supplies to

wrap my ankle before the swelling set in. She was kind and I nearly felt bad about tricking her.

The husband watched me closely, looking for any signs that I was dangerous. I let a few more tears glide down my cheeks and it seemed to alleviate any fears he had.

The wife sat with me, ordering her husband to fetch me some water. He reluctantly turned and walked toward their kitchen. She shifted closer to me and stroked my hair to comfort me, asking me questions about myself.

I gave her a false name and told her my parents were gone. Making her believe I was working day-to-day to earn money for food was easy. She believed every word I said as I teared up on her couch.

I leaned back against the arm of the couch and settled in, as if grateful to be somewhere warm and clean for the time being. When she asked me to spend the night, I declined.

She insisted I let her feed me before I made any decisions. They allowed me to eat their food and made sure I was comfortable. The couple moved to the kitchen to speak to one another and I stood from my resting place and pathetically tried to escape without them noticing, not wanting to be an imposition. I intentionally let them catch me hobbling away and they forced me back inside where I would spend the night.

It was glorious to sleep on a couch again. The last

time I had spent the night in a home was when I trained with Brittella. I sank into an easy sleep, certain I had nothing to fear from the couple. I had played on their every trigger. The list that Lowell gave me had helped immensely to know which tricks to use.

The couple had never had children of their own, but the wife had a soft spot for them, and her husband had a soft spot for her. When *she* decided to take me in, he did as she wanted.

Morning came and I found myself awake before either of them rose. I stayed nestled on the couch, peeking out from under my nearly-closed lashes. My eyes searched the room until I found several places I wanted to check for the lock.

I ate when they offered me breakfast, the warm food tasting like Heaven. I nearly felt bad for deceiving them, but then I remembered what Lowell had told me they had done. They were aiding our enemy and damaging Lowell's plans. I couldn't understand how any group would work against people that were working to bring down our corrupt government, but still, they were.

Later, when the husband left for work, the wife let me rest awhile on my own as she attended to her laundry outside. I immediately sprang in to action, checking the areas I had isolated as possible lock locations. I focused on the window, watching her every move as I raced around the room.

On the fourth try, I found what I was looking for. Hidden behind a false wall, there was a lock. I inserted the key and it clicked open. Reaching inside, I pulled out the contents and shoved them into my hidden pouch on the inside of my dress skirt.

I settled myself back down, then pretended to struggle to get back up almost immediately as the wife walked into the room.

"Are you leaving, dear?"

"Yes, I have to work, but thank you so much for your graciousness. I would have been lost without you."

I allowed her to fawn and fret over me for a few moments before she insisted I take a meal with me. She watched as I hobbled away, never knowing what I had done. I was certain I saw tears in her eyes as I rounded the final corner out of her sight.

For a woman who had known me for less than a day, I had certainly managed to attach myself to her. Perhaps I really *was* ready for whatever Lowell had planned for me.

Chapter 9

Once I made it to the woods, I left my fake limp behind and picked up my pace back to the temporary campsite. When I heard the snap off to my right I froze.

"Hello, little girl," a voice said. I knew I was in trouble. "Where are you off to this fine day?"

Without looking back, I broke into a run. I heard several sets of footsteps following me. I was grateful I had several yards on them but they started to gain speed.

I searched for a tree to climb. If I could reach the top, I could move from tree to tree faster than they could follow me. Unfortunately, I found no such option, the trees being too far spaced out in those woods.

One man caught up with me, and I dove at a tree branch. As he moved to wrap his arms around my waist, I flung myself upward, lifting my feet so he hit nothing but empty space. He crashed to the ground and I landed on top of him, intentionally digging my heels into his back as I pushed off of him.

With his knife in my hand, I turned and whirled it at the oncoming men. It found its mark and sank into the lead man's shoulder. He skidded to a stop, hindering the other men as he thrashed to remove it from his flesh.

The mercenaries advanced on me, intent on gaining their prize. If caught, I would be sold to the soldiers to be sent to the camps. The reward was enough to make the men vicious and relentless.

Knowing I could no longer outrun them, I turned to face them. They weren't expecting me to stop, and the surprised moment gave me just enough time to knock out the man closest to me.

A second man tackled me, pinning me to the ground.

"This one is a fighter," he grinned at his only remaining companion.

"Get her up, let's go," the second man commanded.

They struggled to get me to my feet as I ferociously fought against them. My hand found a branch and I brought it to the first man's head, a painful crack echoing in the forest.

I swung the branch toward the second man,

connecting with such force that it shattered the branch. I ran. I dared one glance back, but the men were not following me. Rather, they were staggering to their feet, trying to get their bearings.

I had never run so fast in my life. I threw myself into the camp and screamed that the men may be following me. A wall of our men formed, ready for the mercenaries to approach. When they did, their fate was sealed.

My heartbeat pounded in my ears and all I could feel were the jarring effects of my feet crashing against the ground and my heart beating against my chest as I ran further into the camp.

I slammed against Shadoe as he stepped into my path, ready to catch me.

"Where's Lowell?" I shouted, struggling to get by him.

"Slow down, Lur." He tried to calm me, but I pushed forward out of his grasp.

"Where is he?" I whipped around, running backward so I could face him.

"Over there." He pointed.

I turned and ran, feet still flying.

I knew I was safe, I was back with the fold and there was no reason to fear those men any longer. I wasn't afraid, but the adrenaline from the chase still coursed through my body and I needed to work it out.

In my bag, I held the final piece, the last part of the plan before Lowell would tell me everything. It had been years waiting for this moment; years of training, years of waiting, and now finally, *finally*, I would know why I had to do it all.

Lowell's eye darted to me as I crashed into view. I didn't bother to hide my footfall; I wanted him to know I was approaching. He immediately sent away the men he was talking to and waited for me to draw near enough that he didn't have to shout.

"Did you…?" he began.

"It's here," I gasped, cutting him off. "It's here."

His face radiated with what I could only conclude was absolute joy as he stretched out his hand to me.

Opening the pouch on my hip, I carefully took out the papers I had worked so hard to protect, even through the fight. I knew I was smiling, and tried to suppress my grin.

He appraised me for a moment before taking the papers from my hand. The glint in his eyes told me he thought I was ready to take on the mission he had been grooming me for.

I waited as he opened the papers, eyes glancing over them. He thumbed through the small stack of pages. The way his eyes darted suggested he was looking for something specific, but they lingered just long enough to confirm he wanted to read every word scribbled in his hands.

I felt Shadoe step up behind me, his presence having become so well known to me, that I was certain I would always be able to tell when he was near. He hovered just behind my shoulder, not near enough to touch me, but enough for his heat to warm my arm.

He let out a short, tiny breath just forceful enough to send my below waist length hair dancing. For a moment, I wanted to close my eyes and tilt my head up to feel the slight breeze linger in the air as it caressed my face and moved my golden locks, but I remained still, terrified that if I moved, I might break the trance Lowell was in as he digested the information on the papers I had acquired.

Lowell looked up and nodded to Shadoe. As Shadoe stepped forward, everything in me sank. Once again, I was to be left out.

Stepping forward, I opened my mouth to speak, but Shadoe silenced me with a barely noticeable shake of the head. I was commanded to wait.

They walked away, leaving me alone. Perhaps I would never be as important as Lowell said I would be; Shadoe certainly was though.

Chapter 10

One week passed without a word from Lowell. Shadoe refused to speak about their meeting.

A second week and I put aside any hopes of knowing.

A third week and stories started to surface about the people we would be fighting against. I even heard drunken tales of them really being wild animals, ravaging the people working against the Society from the safety of the woods. I didn't put much faith in these tales, nor would I believe anything until it came from Lowell himself.

I worked my hair back into a long braid that traveled the length of my back. It was warm, and I wanted it out of my way as I trained. Venturing into the woods, I carried a few extra knives with me, wrapped tightly in a carrier slung across my back.

Finding a tree deep in the heart of the woods and far from prying eyes, I released them one after the other. They found their marks almost every time. When they all rested in the trunk of the trees, I slipped low to the ground, resting against a large rock.

Sitting, I waited for clarity.

I knew Lowell's mission was important: we needed to stop the Society. What I couldn't understand was how long we had to wait to make any advancements on Lowell's plan. I had been with Lowell's fold for so long that, I couldn't even remember what it was like to live in my aunt's house. I had known about Lowell's master plan since my arrival, and still, I knew no details. My training was complete, my entire life had been planned, and still I sat in the middle of the forest, alone and waiting.

"Must you lurk, Shadoe?" I asked, finally.

"You're getting better at this, Lur."

"I've been good at this for a long time now, Shadoe," I corrected as he took a seat near me.

"He's going to tell you soon, you know."

"I'm sure he will," I replied absentmindedly.

"It's happening soon, Lur. Very soon—" He glanced at me long enough to make eye contact before looking back to the knives in the bark across from us.

"You're vital to this. If you fail, we all fail."

"How reassuring," I sniped.

"Pull it together, Lur," he suddenly shouted, whipping toward me. "We need a fighter, not some little girl. You're better than this, so stop sulking and pull it together."

"Well, excuse me for wanting to spend some time as weak little *Auluria* and not trained fighter *Lur*!" I spit back at him, feeling my anger rising.

"You *are* a fighter, *Auluria*. You haven't been a weak little girl in *years* and you know it. Don't go soft on us now. *Pull it together*. Prove to Lowell, and to me, that you can do this."

He was on his feet and walking toward the knives in the trees. Knowing what was coming, I ducked behind the rock I had been leaning against and pulled my last remaining knife out of my boot.

He turned and flung a knife at me, just as I released mine. It caught his sleeve and pinned his arm to the tree. I heard the fabric rip as he pulled away, muttering unkind words.

His knife had been sent off course when mine collided with his sleeve and it clattered against the rock. I scooped it up in case he tried again. He didn't.

He glared at me for a moment before walking over to me and transferred the knives into my arms. Slowly, I put them back into the carrier I laid out on top of the rock.

Shadoe walked away without another word. I nearly

followed him, but decided against it. I would be attached to Shadoe for the rest of my life; there was no need to spend all of my time following his leadership.

After a few moments, I started back toward the camp. All of nature seemed to guide my steps as I slowly made my way back. By the time I reached the fold, my anger had dissipated.

I put the weapons away in my tent before wandering to the edge of the camp.

"Well, if it isn't the pickpocket," an eager voice shouted.

"Leave me alone, Locust," I said, brushing past him.

"What's the matter, having a lover's quarrel?" He grinned. "Because I can help with that."

The girl sitting near him frowned. She looked ready to slit his throat, and I'm sure if she thought Lowell would let it slide, she would have.

I turned and walked away from where they were sitting. I had never taken the time to be social with most of Lowell's people and I wasn't about to start at that point. I made it half way around the perimeter before I heard people starting to pack.

"What's going on?" I asked a red haired young man.

"We're leaving. Second to last stop before we enact the plan." His voice radiated excitement.

I nodded and started off to my own tent. The center

of camp was crowded as young people darted back and forth getting in the way.

I made it back to my tent and gathered my belongings. Within minutes I was packed and had my tent down and ready to be moved.

Shadoe kept his distance as we walked. I knew he was keeping an eye on me, but he was far enough behind me that I didn't have to see or think about him.

I watched as perfect, blonde Anetta attached herself to Lowell's side, forcing the other girls away. They huffed as they slipped away. Anetta giggled as Lowell talked to her. I was surprised she was still hanging on to him after all this time.

Walking gave me time to think—but I had no desire to think. Instead, I tried to focus on my surroundings. I memorized every tree, every cloud, every star that eventually forced its way into the darkening sky.

A cool wind swept back my hair and made me shudder. The walk took an exceptionally long time. It was the next afternoon before we finally settled in a hidden field far from the town.

I slowed my pace near the end of the trip, falling to the back of the group, not wanting to be surrounded by the fold. Once they were distracted by setting up their tents, I slipped away into the trees.

When I neared the town, something inside of me sparked. Recognition.

I had grown up in that town, many lifetimes ago. My aunt's house was nestled in the far end of the town, still close enough to the center to have access to food, but far enough away that prying eyes weren't a terrible plague.

I had to see it. The house.

When I arrived, I waited down the street, watching for signs of new owners. When I was satisfied that I was alone, I crept toward the building. The windows were dirty, but I could tell the house was not being used.

I assumed Lowell had kept it under his control, so I pried the door open and stepped inside. It was almost as I had left it on the day Lowell came for me.

The couch still sat against the same wall. The table in the kitchen had been moved in what I assumed must have been an effort to facilitate the meetings I knew Lowell must have occasionally held there in the infrequent times he had visited the home since I left.

My room was tiny, barely a closet, but the bed still sat, waiting for the little girl to come back to it. I wanted desperately to throw myself into its painfully comforting holds and stay there until I was a child again.

I breathed in the dust-saturated air and stifled a cough. Despite its latent appearance, that place was the last time I felt cared for. I was grateful to Lowell for taking me in and training me, but at least with my aunt I felt… Like I had some real human contact.

Going back to the couch, I removed a sheet and

settled myself onto the bare cushions. Throwing my hands over the armrest on one side, I relaxed my head down until I was cradling my face in my arms.

Sleep came quickly, deeply, and desperately.

The next morning, I expected to find myself being dragged back to the camp by one of Lowell's men, but no one came for me. I was sure Lowell must have known where I was; Lowell was aware of everything it seemed.

Making my way to the back of the house, I found the trap door that led down into the earth. Lowell had insisted we have such a hiding place when his mother was still alive. He installed it long before I lived with my aunt, but only toward the end of my stay with her did I know of its existence.

Crawling down the steps into the ground, I felt the temperature change immediately. The cool earth gave off a damp smell and made me wrinkle my nose.

I had hoped to find Lowell had kept the secret place stocked with food, but when I swept my head from side to side, I discovered it to be empty. Climbing back out, I closed the door and hid it once more.

Outside, people had begun to trade and sell their goods. I watched as two of Lowell's men slipped through the crowd and met a third man: one of our spies. I kept out of sight, hoping they wouldn't report back to Lowell.

I wasn't worried about being recognized in the town; it had been so long since any of them had seen me. Most never knew who I was to begin with; my aunt tried to keep us as far from the public eye as possible knowing the dangers, especially for a young girl.

I recognized a few faces as I worked my way through the crowd, but no one that stood out. Finding food, I paid for it, and started back toward my aunt's home.

I ate as I walked, ducking my head low so as not to draw attention. When I heard the scream, I was so shocked I nearly dropped my last bite of bread.

I looked up just in time to see a young girl being pulled down the street. Several men surrounded her. They clamped their hands around her mouth to muffle her cries. The Society guards dragged her away as she fought against them.

I lurched forward, willing myself to run to her aid. Before I could move, they dropped her dead body to the ground. She had struggled too much and her movements caused them to restrain her to the point of snapping her neck. Her lifeless body toppled to the ground with a heart-wrenching thud.

As they looked up, I darted behind a corner. All I could think of was that despite the fact that she was dead, at least she wasn't taken to those horrible camps. She was free now.

Once inside my aunt's house, I closed the door and took a post at the window. Watching, I waited for the men to come for me. When I felt it was safe, I made my way further into the house.

If Lowell created the secure room, he probably hid other things in the house too.

Moving methodically from one room to the next, I forced thoughts of the dead girl out of my head. I searched each room, finding several hiding places, all of which were empty.

The Society did that to her. They caused her death. They need to be destroyed.

My hands brushed along the walls, looking for anything irregular about them. The floors were an obvious place to search. Inside of cabinets and within doors, I found deceptive recesses that Lowell must have once used to conceal items.

I will do whatever it takes to stop the Society. For that girl... For all of us.

Lowell proved to be very good at hiding things. I found twenty-three unique hiding places in my aunt's house.

If only we could hide from the Society so easily.

I covered up the hidden places once more, leaving them to rest in the peace my presence had disturbed. I hid one knife in the hardest of the places to find, deep in the heart of the house. Should I ever need to return, it would be there, waiting for me.

Sleep eluded me that night. The moon glistened off the floor, bouncing through the window and cascading around the walls. It illuminated my thoughts and brought clarity to the muddled confusion.

By morning, I knew I would have to return to Lowell's camp. I would do as he asked, knowing how important it was to free the people from the Society's rule.

Once Lowell had completed his master plan, he would set the Society straight, and we could fight off the villains on the other side of the wall that had been terrorizing us. Lowell would make things right, and Shadoe and I would help him succeed.

I slipped into town that afternoon, hoping to gather intelligence for Lowell before my return. I was certain he'd be upset over my absence and I needed to make up for it.

I followed a set of Society soldiers as they made their way through the town, taking what they wanted and forcing people out of their way. I thought once to send a knife into the back of their heads, but I had never been able to handle such disregard for life.

Following them, I watched them enter a tavern late that evening. I had hoped to find where they went, but I knew they would offer no further information to me beyond those walls.

I slept soundly on the pathetic couch in my aunt's house, waking early and making my way back to the tavern in time to see the same two men stumble out. Several others cast them disgusted looks, knowing soldiers weren't supposed to behave like that.

By the end of the day, I had spoken to several men from the town, learning more about the soldier's schedules. I tested their knowledge and returned to my aunt's home with several stolen Society weapons to prove the point.

Knowing it would be my last night with a real couch, I slept early. The crickets sang as I slipped into a fitful sleep. Thoughts of Lowell's master plan and what it might entail invaded my dreams. Early in the morning I sank into a comfortable rest.

"Auluria?" Lowell said, appearing in front of me. "I think we should talk."

I sat up, staring at the only remaining family I had left. Of course he had known where I had been.

"Things are progressing and we're ready to start activating our plan. Are you ready for that?"

"Yes," I answered truthfully. I'd been waiting for this day for a long time.

"Good." He motioned for me to get up and follow him to the kitchen table.

"I'm ready to do whatever you need me to do, Lowell," I informed him as he walked away, giving me enough time to focus myself.

"I have information on the Society soldier's schedules in the town here," I added, making sure he knew I had helpful information for him.

"Good," he called. "We can use that."

When I rounded the corner, I found him already sitting in one of the chairs, papers spread out in front of him.

"It's time we talk about your targets, Auluria," he said, motioning me to sit. "These people are incredibly bad; they're the reason the Society continues to exist. Those papers you procured for us from the house with the lock, gave us their current location."

I met his eyes and saw hatred in them. I steeled myself for the next words out of his mouth as he handed me papers, much like the information I had learned about the couple with the lock I had broken into.

I took the papers without looking at them, focusing on Lowell's bitterly angry words. They came out like venom, laced with vindication.

"It's time we talk about Berwyn Baer and his kid brother."

ACKNOWLEDGMENTS

Thank you all so much for joining me on this trip into Auluria's past. And, yes, that *was* a little glimpse of you-know-who tucked away in there! I figured we'd *all* appreciate that!

Special thanks to my amazing Robins-you all are incredible and I couldn't be more grateful to you all for your willingness to help and support me as my Street Team.

Extra special thanks to Yentl, Jess, Danna, Elissa, Sissy, and Alexis for going above and beyond as my Elites. You all are the best! I can't even tell you how cool you ladies are! You're the most fabulous support system a lady could ask for! *high five* and *confetti*

So much love to Awnna for being so wonderful through this process, Elissa for always stepping up and going above and beyond, and Brenna for putting so much time and effort in to help me out! Thank you, thank you, thank you.

And to you, dearest reader of mine, I thank you for sticking with me. If you're here, that means you've been through Golden and have fallen for this charming little tale of mine and I could not be more thrilled that you're continuing this journey with me. I adore you-I hope you know that!

That being said—reach out. Contact me on social media, send me an email, or chat with me during a live broadcast. I want to be friends! My social media door is always open to you and I'd love to chat and get to know you better! Please don't ever hesitate to reach out!

I can't wait for you to read the sequel to Golden where we see some of these people make new appearances in the Golden tale, and see how some of Auluria's past ends up playing a role in her future. It's going to be magnificent!

Keep reading to find out how to get Golden bonus scenes, to find out how to play interactive games to help Auluria get ready for her mission to see the Baers, get more bonus scenes, and even gain access to Golden filters for your photos and live broadcasts. I might even tell you a bit about the Dov prequel novella inside of the Golden omnibus/boxset that you don't want to miss…the first chapter is on the next page!

Stay inspired,

-K.M.

TEMPERED

THE DOV PREQUEL

"**G**et up," Berwyn sounded angry.

"I'm up," I mumbled, rolling over on the cot. I untangled myself from the sheets, setting my feet on the cold floor.

"We have places to be, baby brother, now let's move," Berwyn chides.

"How are you up before me?" I run my fingers through my hair, working out a couple of knots. "You're never up this early."

"Only when we have a mission."

"We're going on a mission?" I asked, now fully awake.

"Dad has somewhere for us to be today—now, let's go."

"Okay, I'm up, I'm up." I scrambled to get dressed and pull my boots on. "What's the mission?"

"We're going to town," Berwyn said, grabbing a few berries from the bowl on the table. "We have a contact to meet."

"Is Dad coming too?" I hurried to the table to grab something to eat before we left.

"Yes, he wants to introduce us to the contact so that we can run messages for him."

"Ready, boys?" Dad asked, strolling into the room with an easy smile.

We nodded and followed him outside. I grabbed a few berries to take along the way.

The trees were bathed in yellow light. I ducked under the low branches next to my dad as I walked beside him —I was quickly approaching his height. To be fair, neither Berwyn nor I would ever be as tall as Griz Baer was, but I was happy with catching up.

"Apple?" he asked, pulling one down from a branch as we passed.

Berwyn reached up, plucking his own from the tree. I bit into the one my father tossed to me, the flavor making my jaw tingle into my ears—it was *perfect.*

"Where are we headed?" I asked, crunching on another bite of the apple.

"I need to take you two to meet someone today," Dad says, glancing over at Berwyn. "He used to be one of Lowell's contacts, but now that he's taking a step back, I need you two to step up and fill the void."

He put Lowell's probation in a softer light than he should have.

"Have you talked to him recently?" Berwyn asked, looking at our father out of the corner of his eye.

"Yes, we've talked," Dad nodded. "He understands that he needs to stay on course if he wishes to continue working with us to bring down the Society and restore a more peaceful nation. He's been doing well accommodating his restrictions."

Berwyn ducked under a tree branch as we stepped out of the woods. The dirt road was packed down so hard that the dust didn't even kick up as we walk into the town.

People bustled by, trading goods and having conversations. I waved to a guy my age sitting in his father's shop as he worked. Peter and his father secretly worked with our family, acting as our lookouts in the town—one of many.

We wove our way around carts and tables, only stopping once or twice to pick a few supplies up. Berwyn kept a watchful eye on me as if I might wander off, but my father's wink softened the oversight.

"This is Lionel," Dad nodded ahead, waving his hand slightly. "He's your new contact."

Lionel greeted my father warmly as we approached.

"Griz," he said, smiling. "Glad you made it. Lowell still on probation?"

"He is," my father answered. "He's coming around though. I think he just needed to get it out of his system. For now, you're going to be working with my boys. You remember Berwyn and Dov, right?"

"I do. Hello, boys." He smiled politely at us. "It's been quite a while since I've seen either of you. You were both pretty young the last time I was out your way. It's nice to officially meet you again."

"Nice to meet you, Lionel," Berwyn greeted him.

"Let's take a little walk," Lionel said as he turned. "I'll show you our locations for meetings."

He guided us around the town to several places, telling us what signals to watch for at each location so we would know when it was safe to approach. It was nice that he included me as part of the team—usually Berwyn did most of the work because he was older and respected more.

"Dov," my dad pulled me back as Lionel showed Berwyn around. "I know you've been looking to take on more authority in the group. I'd like to expand some of your responsibilities, starting with this. You've been handling quite a bit of the lower-level work with our contacts, but now I want you to start taking on more of our crucial work. I've already started Berwyn, but now it's your turn."

"I'd like that," I answered.

"You've been doing a great job, son," he replied. "I think you have a real talent for this. Silas too. I'd like to give him more responsibility as well. I've already spoken to his father about it. You two make a great team, and I'd like to pair you together for a few missions."

Silas was like a brother to Berwyn and me. The only thing that truly separated us was having different parents. Silas had been with us for as long as I could remember—our mothers were good friends when they were younger.

"That would be great, Dad."

"I need you to pay close attention to this. Lionel will be your brother's contact, but you'll need to meet with him on occasion too. You and Silas are going to be doing more intelligence gathering for me rather than this type of work, but you'll still need to be familiar with it. Think you can handle that?"

"Absolutely," I confirmed. I was beginning to like this trip.

"Good. Pay attention—I'm sending you back here later," he warned me.

I watched everywhere we went, trying to commit it all to memory. *I'd be back soon.*

"Lionel," I greeted him quietly, slipping up next to the man at a stand. He looked at a pile of apples, examining each one before setting them back down.

"Dov, Silas," he responded without looking at us. "Do you have it?"

I took the bag off my shoulder, letting it rest in my hand. Lionel casually reached down and took it from me, shifting it onto his own shoulder after a minute.

"That one, please," he said, pointing to a small basket of apples. "Thanks."

He handed the man money for his purchase and turned to me.

"Well, it's been a few weeks, how do you boys think it's going?" he asked.

"I feel like I've learned a lot," Silas responded. "Griz has been sending us on a lot of missions—I think we've done well."

"I agree," I added. "I feel like I have a much better grasp on doing reconnaissance work. Yesterday, we helped Arin out with a mission."

"That's good," Lionel responded. "Have you seen Peter yet today?"

"We stopped there first. He's actually coming back with us for a few days."

"Dov!" We heard him before we saw him in the crowd.

"Speaking of…" Silas mumbled quietly.

"Dov," Peter was out of breath when he approached me. He breathed heavily as he rested a hand on my shoulder, bent over to try to regulate his oxygen intake. "There's a problem."

"What's wrong?" Lionel asked, taking over.

"Something happened in the next town over," Peter gasped. "I don't know what it is, but my father sent me to find you. They're blaming your father for something. You need to go warn him."

Silas' face matched my own. Lionel gripped my shoulder, turning me to face him.

"Now, listen, Dov. You go find your father, and then send Arin to meet me by the edge of town. I'm going to do some digging today to find out what happened." He turned to Peter. "I want you to go with them and make sure everyone is in a safe location until we know what is going on. I'll send your father after you—don't go back to him."

We nodded.

"Go quickly and don't come back until we know what's happened. Avoid the Society men at all costs," he added. Lionel pushed us down the street, away from the town. "Hurry and don't get caught."

We rushed through the streets as quickly as we could without running. Once we reached the woods, we took off, racing as fast as possible up hills and under low tree branches.

"How bad is this?" I asked when we were far enough away that we wouldn't be overheard.

"Bad," Peter shook his head. "I don't know what happened, but, Dov, they're coming for your dad. I don't think its safe."

I took a deep breath, forcing myself not to stop running to process his words. We'd figure something out—we always did.

"What do you think Griz is going to do?" Silas wondered, darting around a tangled mass of roots sticking out of the ground.

"I don't know, but I think it's a smart idea to get him where the Society can't find him," I replied, using my hand to lift a branch as I fly under it. It snapped back behind me when I let it go.

"That's probably a good idea," Silas commented.

"Where will he go?" Peter asked, trying to keep up with us. He spent most of his life in the town, leaving him without our strict training and physical conditioning. He had done some of it with us, just not to the extent we had been trained.

"We have a few safe houses that we keep for this reason. We've also got the storehouses if we need somewhere else to stay," I informed him. "We have options—Dad has always been prepared."

"I have a feeling you'll be staying with us for a while, Peter," Silas mused as he pulled forward just enough to make Peter work harder to keep up. We were trying to do our best to wait for him, but we needed to get back to the group.

"Can't say it would be the worst thing in the world," Peter tried to grin. "Almost there."

He lowered his head as he pushed forward, trying to make the last bit of the sprint to the storehouse where we would find my father. We burst through doors, causing everyone within a twenty-foot radius to turn to us.

I scanned the crowd, searching for my father and Berwyn. The great Griz Baer leans around Arin to look at me. When he saw the look on my face, he marched over to me, Arin and my brother close behind.

"Peter and his father sent word that there was an incident in the next town over," I reported. "We don't know what is it yet—Lionel was going to look into it—but the Society is blaming you. We were sent to tell you."

My father's face paled.

"We had a mission there today." His voice was low and gravelly, a sign that he was worried. "We need to check on our men."

He moved toward the door, but Silas and I blocked him.

"You can't," I protested. "They're looking for you."

"I'll go," Berwyn volunteered.

I shook my head.

"Lionel said to send Arin," I responded, turning to the tall man. "You need to meet him by the edge of town for a report."

Arin turned to look at my father. After a long pause, Dad released him to go investigate.

"We think you need to stay in a safe house," I proposed. "We can't have the Society catch you before we even know what is going on."

"Dov, I know your heart is in the right place, but I'm not just going to leave our men out there to face the Society on their own." He stooped down to place his hand on my shoulder and looked me in the eyes. "I'll be okay. You wait here with your brother and I'll be back soon."

"I think you need to stay," Berwyn objected. "*I just….you need to stay.*"

Berwyn didn't often have trouble with words, so it got my father's attention.

"You really think so?"

"I do," Berwyn nodded emphatically.

"Sometimes our bodies know things our brains don't, boys. *Sometimes*, you need to listen to that intuition." He took a step back. "We'll wait for Arin to report back."

Relief flooded over me. I watched as he wandered over to a group of people to start informing them of what was going on. I knew he wouldn't take this sitting down—he'd start making a plan immediately.

"At least we got him to stay," Silas murmured next to me.

"*Berwyn* got him to stay," I corrected him, running my hand through my hair.

"Yeah, let's remember that trick next time," Silas smirked.

"Good call," I grin. "Hey, where did Peter go?"

"He's over there talking to the girls," Silas waved in their general direction.

"Oh," I replied, looking down. I shouldn't have been surprised Peter would be taking advantage of spending time with the girls while he was here—he doesn't get to see them often. "Maybe you should go and talk to them too."

He shrugged as if it didn't matter, but it did. I knew Silas had a fondness for one of the girls but hadn't said anything to her yet.

"Maybe *you* should, buddy. *You're* the one they all dote over."

"Yeah," I rolled my eyes. "That's only because I'm Berwyn's brother and Dad's son."

"Probably," he agreed. His face lit up mischievously. If we weren't inside, I would have pummeled him. Too bad he was aware of that too and played into it. "But we've got to find you a girl *somehow*, my friend. *Take what you can get.*"

"Did I just hear you say that you're available, Dov?" a soft voice interrupted the conversation.

"Hi, Kat," Silas greeted Katarina, swinging around. "Long time, no see."

"Hello, Silas," she purred, sidling up next to him. She waved her hand around at the various meetings happening in the room. "You want to tell me what's going on or do I have to flirt with Dov to get it out of you two?"

Silas grinned, having much more fun with the conversation than I was—he wiped the look off his face before answering.

"It looks like one of our missions went sideways, and the Society figured out we were involved. We're waiting to see what happens."

Katarina pulls an apple out of her bag.

"When was the last time you boys ate?" she asked, twisting the apple in her hand. "You two should eat something now, in case you don't have time later."

"What's going on?" Reyla demanded playfully as she approached.

"Something is up and the boys need to eat before they

go running off to handle it," Katarina announced. Silas grew quiet.

"We'll be okay," I supplied, "but thank you, Katarina."

"Fine, be that way." She sashayed away. "But don't say I didn't warn you."

"Okay," I called after her, turning back to Silas. Reyla followed after her friend. "You know, she was probably right."

"So, we'll go find food. It's probably a wise choice for your father to eat too. Let's go grab something for him."

We spend the next hour foraging for food and information.

preorder swag, giveaways, and more, so watch the social media pages carefully for the next scene giveaway.

K.M. Robinson also has bonus scenes and extras from all of her books on
newsletter.kmrobinsonbooks.com

Sign up now for weekly emails with special bonuses, extras, live broadcasts replays and upcoming dates, events, coloring pages, games, introductions to new authors+live broadcasts with them, and more.

WORLD PORTALS

Ready to learn exclusive facts about The Golden Trilogy and other K.M. Robinson Series?

World Portals are now available on
www.kmrobinsonbooks.com

Learn behind the scenes facts, watch videos, play games, check out our book filters, find out where to get bonus scenes, view fan art, and get access to other secrets we've hidden away inside the World Portals on the website.

The World Portals are constantly changing and information is being taken away and added all the time, so check back frequently for new content!

GOLDEN MISSION INTERACTIVE GAME

Auluria is being sent on one last mission before Lowell and Shadoe send her to destroy Dov and Berwyn Baer and she needs your help. Are you ready to assist Goldilocks and locate the Baers?

This interactive, choose-your-own-adventure game is played through Facebook messenger so you never miss a mission. Played over the course of one-two days, you and Auluria will go on several missions to discover the location of her next target and then you can go back into the story and see how your actions lead up to everything in the book.

PLAY THE GAME

at

goldenmission.kmrobinsonbooks.com

Auluria will meet with you few times for different missions over the course of a few days, with gaps of time in between so you can "complete the missions" and report back. She will be in touch!

Have fun running missions to help Auluria find Dov and Berwyn and then go back in the story to see how your choices directly affect them in the story.

Want to get your hands on some incredible Facebook filters for Golden? Now you have the ability to get filters for the story, characters, etc right inside your phone.

You can use these on your photos, profile pictures,

videos, and live broadcasts. All you have to do is like my author page and they will automatically show up in your filters!

I've even taken these clips and put them on Instagram Stories by saving them to my phone and uploading them to Instagram.

Visit www.facebook.com/kmrobinsonbooks to grab these filters for your photos, videos, and broadcasts! Bonus points for tagging me @kmrobinsonbooks so I can see how you're supporting The Golden Trilogy.

ABOUT THE AUTHOR

K.M. Robinson is a storyteller who creates new worlds both in her writing and in her fine arts conceptual photography. She is a marketing, branding and social media strategy educator who is recognized at first sight by her very long hair. She is a creative who focuses on photography, videography, couture dress making, and writing to express the stories she needs to tell. She almost always has a camera within reach. Visit her at her website: www.kmrobinsonbooks.com

CONNECT ON SOCIAL MEDIA

facebook.com/kmrobinsonbooks

instagram.com/kmrobinsonbooks

twitter.com/kmrobinsonbooks

Get free excerpts and full novels from K.M. Robinson at
excerpt.kmrobinsonbooks.com

ALSO BY K.M. ROBINSON

The Golden Trilogy

Book One: Golden

Forged: A Golden Novella

Book Two: Locked

Book Three: Edge

The Complete Series Boxset/Omnibus with Tempered: an exclusive bonus novella

The Jaded Duology

Book One: Jaded

Book Two: Risen

The Complete Series Boxset/Omnibus with exclusive epilogue

The Siren Wars Saga

Book One: The Siren Wars

Book Two: Darker Depths

Book Three: Beyond The Shores

Origins of the Siren Wars: Prequel Novella

Book Four: Forbidden Waters (coming soon)

The Legends Chronicles

Along Came A Spider: A Prequel Novelette

And They'll Come Home: A Prequel Novelette

The Archives of Jack Frost Series

The Revolution of Jack Frost

The Redemption of Jack Frost (coming soon)

Stealing Steam Series

Book One: Lions and Lamps

Book Two: Pistons and Prisoners

Book Three: Railcars and Rulers

Top Hats and Telegraphs: A Prequel Novella

The Complete Series Boxset/Omnibus with Vambraces and Victories: an exclusive bonus novella

Virtually Sleeping Beauty: A Novella Retelling

The Goose Girl and The Artificial: A Novella Retelling

The Sinking: A Little Mermaid Novella Retelling

Cindrill: A Cinderella Assassin Novella Retelling

Sugarcoated: A Hansel and Gretel's Witch Novella Retelling

Blood Is Silent: A Red Riding Hood Circus Retelling

JADED: BOOK ONE OF THE JADED DUOLOGY

If the only way to stay alive was to convince your new husband not to murder you and make it look like an accident, could you do it?

At eighteen, Jade shouldn't have to be forced to marry the son of her father's enemy as part of a revenge plot for a failed rebellion. When she's thrown into the life of being the wife of the Commander's son and heir, her only hope for survival is convincing Roan Diamond to actually fall in love with her so that he doesn't kill her on his father's wishes.

While a dutiful son, Roan shouldn't have to trick his new wife into believing his family accepts her, but as the only one in a position to make the country believe Jade is part of their family, he will do what he has to before his family murders his young bride and makes it look like an accident to get back at Jade's father.

With half the country trying to protect Jade and the other half oblivious to the atrocities committed at the Commander's hand, it's a race to see who will win at a deadly game of cat and mouse.

One chooses life. One chooses death. In the midst of chaos, only one will succeed.

Now available!
Learn more about The Jaded Duology at
jadedinfo.kmrobinsonbooks.com

THE SIREN WARS: BOOK ONE OF THE SIREN WARS SAGA

War has hovered around the kingdom of Scylla for generations ever since the original sirens left the mer collection generations ago after nearly drowning the human prince. Over the years, select mermaids from the royal bloodline have been trained as spies to work for the reigning kings and queens, keeping the collection safe from sirens and humans.

Celena and her partner, Merrick, work covertly for the royals—not even her twin brother knows. When they discover the sirens have broken through the barriers the mer set up to keep the sirens out, Celena and her friends must race to the old kingdom of Metten to stop them from starting a war within their borders.

When she's dragged to the surface, Celena realizes that the war above the waters is as deadly as the one below the waves—and sacrificing herself may be the only way to protect her family.

The Siren Wars have only just begun.

Available now!

Learn more about The Siren Wars Saga at sirenwarsinfo.kmrobinsonbooks.com

LIONS AND LAMPS: BOOK ONE OF THE STEALING STEAM SERIES

All wishes require sacrifice...*are you willing to pay the price?*

Cyra spent the last seven years being trained to steal an airship in a brutal competition that leaves the victor with millions. Last year, she won.

Aladdin spent the past year fighting to get enough money to take his mother away from Horallen after his father was murdered. Now, his evil uncle Kacper wants to force him into the competition and straight to his death inside the Collection Cave.

When Aladdin discovers a genie said to have been banished a century ago, the competition becomes even deadlier, and he knows he can't trust the girl who snuck into the competition this year...but Cyra might not survive his ruthlessness either in a game where only the lion's heart can win.

All wishes require sacrifice, and someone is going to pay the price for the Stourbridge.

Available now!
Learn more about The Stealing Steam Series at
lionsandlampsinfo.kmrobinsonbooks.com

ALONG CAME A SPIDER: THE FIRST PREQUEL NOVELETTE TO THE LEGENDS CHRONICLES

Little Hacker Muffet

sat on her tuffet

destroying her cords and Way.

Along came a hacker named Spider,

who sat down beside her

and frightened his opponent away.

When Fet, one of the most skilled hackers in the Legends, discovers her best friend and leader of her group has been abducted and held for ransom, she must escape unnoticed and find Peep before it's too late.

When Spider, a new recruit training to join her hacker

ring, slips out with her and claims to have a plan to save her friend, Fet is forced to bring him along. As she discovers he's not who he claims to be, she faces grave danger and learns just how deadly a spider bite can be.

Now available!
Learn more about The Legends Chronicles at
acasinfo.kmrobinsonbooks.com

VIRTUALLY SLEEPING BEAUTY

o wake her up, he has to enter the game and help her beat it...

Surely the class president wouldn't illegally over-juice to stay in the virtual reality game citizens are allowed to play for four hours a day, but when Royce's aunt calls in a panic because her goddaughter hasn't left the game yet, his only option is to go inside the game and drag the girl out.

The golden knight quickly discovers the princess' absence in the real world isn't of her own doing—*she's trapped inside the game by unknown forces*—and if she can't escape soon, she could die for real outside of the game. He's even more shocked to discover that Rora outranks him inside of the game, which means she'll have to fight to *protect herself* from the evils locking her inside a dangerous world.

Can Rora and Royce work together to outsmart a vicious queen and evil magician, and defeat digital dragons, or will Rora slowly fade away until there's nothing left but an empty shell and the game ranking she will leave behind?

Now available!

Learn more about Virtually Sleeping Beauty at
vsbinfo.kmrobinsonbooks.com

THE REVOLUTION OF JACK FROST

No one inside the snow globe knows that Morozoko Industries is controlling their weather, testing them to form a stronger race that can survive the fall out from the bombs being dropped in the outside world—all they know is that they must survive the harsh Winter that lasts a month and use the few days of Spring, Summer, and Fall to gather enough supplies to survive.

When the seasons start shifting, Genesis and Jack know something is going on. As their team begins to find technology that they don't have access to inside their snow globe of a world, it begins to look more and more like one of their own is working against them.

. . .

Genesis soon discovers Morozoko Industries, but when a foreign enemy tries to destroy their weather program to make sure their destructive life-altering bombs succeed in destroying the outside world, only one person can shut down the machine that is spinning out of control and save the lives of everyone inside the bunker—Jack.

Now available!
Learn more about The Revolution of Jack Frost at
jackfrostinfo.kmrobinsonbooks.com

THE GOOSE GIRL AND THE ARTIFICIAL

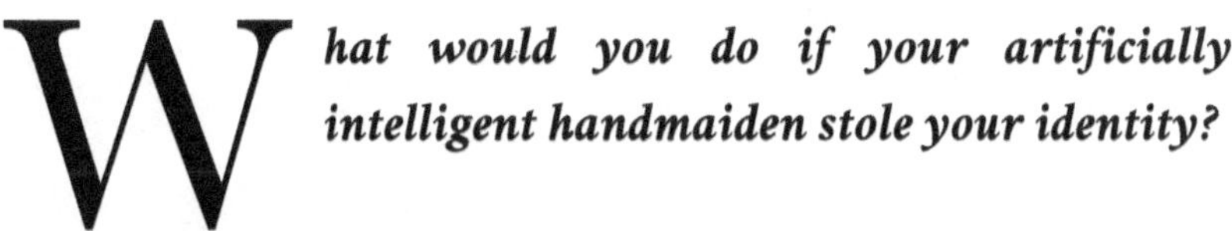

What would you do if your artificially intelligent handmaiden stole your identity?

Threatened by her Artificial, Arta, Princess Goselyn is forced to switch places and pretend she isn't human when she reaches Prince Corinth to negotiate a treaty they both need to be able to take their respective crowns one day. If she doesn't comply, her Artificial, controlled by her evil cousin, will not only kill Goselyn's mother, but Prince Corinth and his father as well.

Can the quiet princess outsmart a machine created to be more intelligent than she is, all while surviving the other

Artificials and robots working against her in the foreign palace, or will Corinth and his father find out and destroy her chance to save them all?

136

Learn more about The Goose Girl and The Artificial at
goosegirlinfo.kmrobinsonbooks.com

THE SINKING

The sea witch wants to silence her, but not for the reason you think.

When a quirky older woman pawns a fancy seashell necklace at her mother's antique shop on the pier, Cara doesn't think much about the story the woman spins about the wearer turning into a mermaid.

On her way home, she accidentally drops the necklace into the ocean and is swept out to sea where she meets— a merman who volunteers to take her to his mother, the sea queen, to help her get her legs back.

. . .

Cara soon learns that it's Quay's eighteen birthday—a day that has been a curse for his family—and is meant to be one for her too. Now she must fight to survive the sea with Quay at her side.

Fans of The Little Mermaid will love this twisted take on the beloved story.

Now available!
Learn more about The Sinking at
thesinkinginfo.kmrobinsonbooks.com

CINDRILL

Cinderella is an assassin out to murder the prince...*but he's hunting her too.*

The nanobots Cindrill's master gives her to use as a mask allow her to slip into the ball wearing a face that isn't hers, but when the assassination attempt goes sideways, Prince Davin doesn't understand why her face changes when he injures her, slicing her foot open around a unique pair of shoes as she runs away.

When Cindrill runs into the prince the next day without her nanobot mask on, he doesn't recognize her, but immediately decides her skills will be useful on his hunt for the would-be-assassin woman who nearly killed his father and his fiancée the night before.

Both are tasked with the job of murdering the other, but things don't quite go as they had planned when Cindrill's master and Davian's fiancée interfere as the two try to decide whether or not to kill the other.

It's hard to recognize a woman when she uses technology to change her appearance, but Cindrill is going to use that to her full advantage as she destroys the prince. **Will either survive?**

Now available!

Learn more about Cindrill at
cindrillinfo.kmrobinsonbooks.com

SUGARCOATED

Hansel and Gretel's witch was actually on their side...

Annika's job is to create a cake to match the candy-colored rooftops, nightly firework shows, and daily parades ending in unexpected executions for the mad king's ball, but her true mission is to sneak a thirteen-year-old assassin into the palace using her gift of illusions.

Hansel's job is to protect his little sister, Gretel, once she assassinates King Levin and ends the destruction in Candestrachen, using his power over light to rescue the young girl from the chaos her influence over life and death will create.

· · ·

When the entire forest reconstructs itself under Gretel's command while trying to save herself from a king's guard, Hansel and Annika must put their feelings aside and ensure their plan holds true—even if it means one of them has to sacrifice themselves to protect the mission.

Her illusions were meant to save her….but not everyone will survive the assassination attempt.

Learn more about Sugarcoated at
sugarcoatedinfo.kmrobinsonbooks.com

BLOOD IS SILENT

R ed Riding Hood is a circus aerialist and the
wolf is ready to cage her.

Sienna has grown up working for the circus, dangling off
her signature red silks every night. Her grandmother has
been known to wander off to train new acts for their
boss, but when Sienna tries to find her to bring her back
to the show, she doesn't expect the dashing and
dangerous Elijah to join her.

When they finally find Grandma Ida has been trans-
formed deep in the heart of the woods, Sienna will stop

at nothing to save her—but the wolf has her right where he wants her, and she won't be able to escape his claws.

She was told not to go into the woods alone.

Now available!

Learn more about Blood Is Silent at
bloodissilentinfo.kmrobinsonbooks.com